Forgotten Past

D.P. Pankratz

Pankratz

Forgotten Past is a work of eyewitness accounts regarding, (The House God Damned, based on five individuals who wish to remain silent.) (The Sanatorium story) is partly based on one man's POV experience at the Saskatoon Sanatorium, while other parts were embellished to create a full story. Other than the fore mentioned, names, places, incidents, all other people, places, and incidents are fictitious, and products of the authors imagination. Any resemblance to actual persons, living or dead are coincidental.

Published in the United States by Lulu.com

LIBRARY AND ARCHEIVES CANADA CATALOGING-IN-PUBLICATION DATA

Pankratz, Perry (Perry P.)

Forgotten Past/D.P.Pankratz

Forgotten Past: a collection /D.P. Pankratz

ISBN 978-1-9994821-4-5

Printed in the United States of America

Lulu.com

First Edition

<u>Dedications</u>

To my loving wife, Teresa. Twenty-nine years together, such a long journey we've traveled. Thank you for sticking with me.

A couple big thank you(s) to some of the most influential people in my life…

Sam Stinn, a great editor who's been with me through thick and thin for the past year. A caring individual who I respect greatly.

The two teachers that helped me blossom into a writer, Greg Stark, and Jeanette Wiens-Peckham. These two individual people influenced me to write beyond what I ever thought I could. Thank you, and all the other teachers that helped in various other ways.

I would also like to thank anyone I may have missed. My many friends who stood by me in my darkest of days, and the lightest ones as well. Strangers, who are now friends with my utmost respect.

A huge thank you to the readers of these stories, I hope they inspire you in some way to enjoy life, or that one person you haven't talked to for years.

Thank each and every one of you.

Pankratz

<u>Contents</u>

The Furnace

May 12, 1907.

It had been a long year since I left my unforgiving family in Spartanburg, South Carolina. My parents told me I'd amount to no more than moss on a log, and all because I didn't want to participate in the annual Belle of the Ball. I didn't need to be paraded in front of hundreds to know my worth, so I hit the road running and never turned back once. Everywhere I've been since that day has led me to where I'm headed. No man has laid his hands upon me and lived to tell the tale; I've left a trail of bodies longer than the road I've traveled thus far.

Walking down this unfamiliar stretch of road, I look up as the clouds float by gracefully. I try to enjoy the various birds chirping their songs amongst the thousands of trees clustered on either side of the road as an unknown middle-aged man begins to follow me, trying to strike up a conversation.

"What brings you out this way, my lady? I've never see you round these parts before, are you lost? What's your name? Cat got your tongue?" he asks, not waiting for a response in between questions.

I glare towards him out of the corner of my eye. "Mary Lou Bell," I reply, irritated, trying to walk a little faster. He speeds up to keep pace with me and continues to talk with a suspicious tone I'm quite familiar with.

"That's a pretty name, Mary. I'm Kyle. You have lovely brown curly hair, and that dress suites a fine lass like yourself..."

I roll my eyes and he gets a little closer. "Thank you!" I answer, annoyed, as I move to my right a few steps,

"I'm heading down to Princeton, West Virginia. Where are you headed?"

I glance towards him and see an excited, lustful look in his eyes. "I'm going wherever my feet carry me," I respond, getting more irritated by the moment.

"You're funny, but seriously. Where you headed? I'll follow you. You're too young to be out in this wilderness by yourself."

Knowing I have to do something, I stop dead in my tracks. "Look here, mister. I'll be fifteen in a month. I don't need a chaperone to look after me. I've been on my own for a year now and have my own plans. Go where you're headed, and I'll go elsewhere," I blurt out.

He shakes his head and laughs, "You don't even have a gun to protect yourself. What do you plan to do? Charm them?"

"Don't worry about me," I respond, glaring, "just go about your business."

I continue walking, holding my sack, but Kyle continues to follow me. "Look here, Mary," he says, grabbing my arm. "I have never been so insulted by someone in my life. I'll show you what could happen to you."

He pushes me, and I fall to the ground, watching as he undoes his suspenders and gets on top of me. My fists fly at him, but he leans against my ear and whispers, "Don't worry, Mary. I'll teach you good!"

He holds my left arm as he lifts my dress. With my other hand, I jab my finger in his eye. As it oozes, he jumps off me, screaming in pain and holding his face. I wipe the dirt off my dress and walk over to the edge of the road, picking up a good-sized rock. When I walk back, he's on his knees, screaming and swaying back and forth.

"Guess you showed me alright. I suppose I owe you a reward for your deed. I was always taught a deed should never go unanswered," I state, coldly.

"You blinded me! Why in God's name did you do that?" he shouts.

Grasping the rock tighter, I step behind him and raise it above my head. "Here's your reward!" I yell, bringing the rock down on his head, making a crunching sound. The back of his head starts bleeding, and he slumps to the ground, twitching. I drop the rock with a thud and pick up my sack. "Nice talking with you, Kyle. Behave yourself."

After a while of walking, I come to a sign that reads "Old Devil's Road." Standing at the fork in the road, I look at both roads. Old Devil's Road looks darker and more adventurous, piquing my interest. I head down the road until I reach a huge red brick building. I stop, staring at the factory-like building, when a man behind me shouts, "Watch yourself, young lady!"

Turning, I see a wagon coming up behind me. I move to the side and the man tips his hat as he turns towards the building. I catch a glance at the back of the wagon and see Kyle laying on top of another body. I run after the wagon into the building and ask to see someone in charge.

Forgotten Past

A six-foot burly man with a beard full of soot comes towards me, holding his suspenders and glaring. "Yes? Can I help you, young lady?"

"Yes, I'd like a job," I reply.

He rubs his beard and grumbles as he answers slightly puzzled, "Do you know what we do here, ma'am?"

"I can take a good guess,"

"What's your name, child?"

"Mary Lou Bell, sir, and I am a hard worker."

"Well, Mary Lou, I believe you may just be what we need. Come with me and I'll show you where you'll be working. The pay is two dollars a day, and you cannot leave until the last one is cremated. Can you handle that?"

I nod and the man grins at me as we walk down to the basement.

"Great! My name is Fred Delbarton, and I own this crematorium. I see a spark in your eyes, and it reminds me of the one I had in my eyes when I first started."

We walk to the end of the hall where a man is scraping out a furnace. Going into a huge room, I look around and see a wooden barrel of water and a huge bin of coal beside a long metal stick on fire. There's a man that appears to be scraping what looks like an oven made of brick and metal.

"ANDY!" Mr. Delbarton shouts.

The man immediately stops raking and turns around, his face covered with soot as he replies hurriedly, "Yes, sir?"

"Andy, I'm going to have to let you go."

"Why? I've never let you down..." Andy replies, looking puzzled.

Mr. Delbarton turns and looks towards me, then back at Andy and answers, "I'm sorry, Andy. One thing I've learned in the course of my life is to never pass by an opportunity that crosses your path. This young lady here will be your replacement."

Andy looks at me confused at first, and then starts laughing, "But she's a girl, sir! She'll never handle this furnace."

"I can handle it!" I shout, watching as Andy bends over laughing even harder. Before I can defend myself further, Mr. Delbarton grabs the rake from Andy and throws it across the room. He picks Andy up by the overalls and throws him into the furnace, slamming the door to muffle his screams.

"You want to be a disrespectful ass? I'm going to let Mary teach you a far more valuable lesson than I can. Here's the deal, Andy… if Mary Lou fries your sorry ass, the job is hers. If she doesn't, you're still fired. Let's see what you can do, Mary Lou."

He steps back from the furnace and I look at him, shocked. Mr. Delbarton grins as he watches me spin the wheel. His smile grows as Andy continues to bang on the door.

"You're doing great, but there are two pieces missing," he states, pointing to the coal bin and the torch nearby.

I grab a shovel full of coal and pour it in the chamber next to the furnace. Once I shovel a couple of heaps inside, I grab the torch and place it into the hole at the bottom. There's an explosion as the coal ignites, and I close the door. Andy's screams continue.

"You're hired! After about six to eight hours he'll be cremated, and you'll use this rake to scrape him out of there."

"Thank you! I promise I won't let you down," I answer.

"I know you won't. Once you get accustomed to the furnace, I'll teach you everything else about this place. I have a good feeling you'll be taking over when my turn comes to be placed in the furnace. I can't think of anyone else I would rather see owning this place."

"Really? I would love to own this place. It's beautiful."

It's been thirteen years since I started here. Mr. Delbarton has mentored me, and today I have the honor of cremating him, as per his wishes. I now own the crematorium, and despite the many who disagree with his decision, I plan on keeping up with Mr. Delbarton's high standards.

I walk towards the furnace room through a crowd of jeers. I glare at them as I pass. Walking up to the furnace, I see Mr. Delbarton's face peaceful and at rest. I tear up as I close the door.

"Are you ready, Mary Lou?" Fred Jr. asks, standing by the coal bin.

I nod as he shovels the coal into the next chamber. Putting the shovel down, he grabs the torch and glances at me before stopping. "I can't, Mary Lou. You knew him best. You should do the honors."

Seeing the sincerity in his eyes, I take the torch from his hand and place it inside as an explosion of fire erupts. I stand back as the fire roars.

"He was a good man. He will be sorely missed," Fred Jr says.

"Yes, he was... he is already missed," I reply, wiping my eyes and turning to walk past the hoard of people once more.

I head up to my new office on the second floor. There's a mess of papers thrown about, and I pick up every last page. I notice the book of people owing Mr. Delbarton is missing but smile as I'm reminded of one particular thing he told me years ago.

"Remember, Mary Lou. Always have everything written in triplicate. Only leave the junk in a place everyone can find it."

I laugh as I whisper to myself, "You're a smart man. I'm sure one of the worker's friends owes you. Never fear, they'll pay for this. With interest."

I sit in the office until the last man leaves for the night before walking into another room where a picture of Mr. Delbarton hangs. I open the floorboard underneath the picture and pull out the debts book. Carrying it back to the office, I thumb through every name listed.

The next morning, I gather everyone outside the crematorium to make an important announcement. I watch as everyone stands there, mumbling amongst themselves.

"Thank you everyone for coming out in this rain. I will try to keep it short. As you all have noticed, I have hired extra men recently and I'm sure you have noticed they're not doing your jobs," I state.

"Why did you hire them? What are they here for anyways?" a man in the back shouts.

"I'm glad you asked. See, these men are my new debt collectors. As some of you know, Mr. Delbarton's books were stolen out of the office on the day we laid him to rest. What those people didn't know is that we still have the names of the debtors. Which brings me to the reason we are here today. These men have gathered all the children of these debtors."

"What do you mean, Miss. Bell?"

"In one hour, I will incinerate eleven children. I will leave the names posted to the door, and either the children will burn the debt away or the cash will be on my desk in an hour. At ten o'clock, the furnace will fire up. Thank you, that is all."

I walk away as the angry shouts begin. Some of the men even try charging at me but are quickly stopped.

"Beautiful speech ma'am! I'm sure our arrangement stands at three percent?" Michael asks.

"Thank you, and yes. Everything remains the same. You collect for me and you can dispose of your problems in my furnace twice a month," I reply.

"I'll make sure no one gets in with a gun. I'm sure you have a great many fans."

"I do appreciate a good joke. Yes, I'm sure they'd love to take me apart at the seams. I foresee a long friendship in this deal."

As Michael turns to walk away, an angry man comes in. "Becky Anderson!" he yells.

Michael slams him up against the door, removing the pistol in his belt. He hands it to me as I point towards my office. He leads the way as I follow pointing the gun at his back. I sit at my desk as the man stands in front of me, looking as if he's been crying.

"You said Becky Anderson, correct?" I ask.

"Yes, she is my neighbor, Ralph's, daughter," the man nods.

"And your name?" I ask looking at the ledger.

"Kenneth Demister. How much does he owe? I would like to pay on his behalf as my son Vern and Becky are best friends."

"He is past due by four days on the latest payment. The amount is twelve dollars and thirty-seven cents," I answer.

"I am willing to make the payments for him. He is going through a rough patch. You can take the payments from my wage until he's paid in full."

"That is a kind gift, but I cannot accept. You're already paying for your sister-in-law, Alison, who passed this month. You couldn't handle another payment. I'm sorry, Mr. Demister, but he must pay this bill in full."

I look at my watch after the fourth man pays his bill, and his children are released. I walk down the stairs and pass Emily Brower as I make my way to the seven remaining children that await their futures. As I nod, my newly appointed debt collectors place the screaming children inside the furnace, firing it up. Within minutes, the screams are silenced.

August 24, 1938.

As I make my way into the tavern, thunder crashes through the silence. Seeing the members of the surrounding communities sitting in the corner, I walk over as they stare.

"Are you finally going to stand with us against Mary, William?" Jack asks.

I stop at the table and place my hands on two of their shoulders. "After what I witnessed this evening, yes. I'm ready," I reply, shaking my head.

"What happened this time?" Fred asks.

Forgotten Past

I chug down a shot of whiskey and slam the glass on the table. "She killed her husband in that blasted furnace. I swear she's going crazy!"

"You're only realizing that now?" Bob asks.

"No, I have known for a few months, but these last thirty days... Mary's going off the rails. She's killing all the debtors if they're a day late! She used to give them a week to pay. I just don't know what's going on in her head."

"She's been crazy since she took over that crematorium and burned those children alive!" Jim raises his voice.

"Yes, I know. And perhaps she is. Or, maybe if someone hadn't stolen that ledger in the first place she wouldn't have gone this route?"

"I took that book from her office. You know everyone was struggling to survive. Don't blame my stealing for Mary's mental state!" Craig replies.

"You took that book? Why? Why would you do that? Everyone was struggling, and she knew that. I will blame you. You got my son, Robert, killed because I couldn't pay in that hour!" I shout angrily, lunging at him.

I punch him and blood spurts out of his nose and mouth. I keep punching until someone pulls me off him. "You Bastard!" I scream as they help him to his feet.

"I said don't blame me!" Craig replies, wiping his mouth.

"I will blame you until the day I die. Let me go!" I shout.

I watch as Craig holds a handkerchief to his mouth and walks out the door. Turning to John, my eyes fill with tears. "He killed my boy. She's keeping everything as Mr. Delbarton had it. Craig drove her mad."

"William? Are you still with us?" John interrupts my sobs.

"Yes, let's get this over with," I respond, allowing John to help me to my feet.

We make our way down Old Devil's road, aptly named since Mary Lou Bell took over. Coming to the crematorium, the chimney is blowing dark smoke. Twelve of us head to the basement, where I last saw Mary Lou. "William...? What are you doing here?" She asks, turning around as we enter.

"We've come to finish this once and for all, Mary. It's time for you to get in there and burn for everything you have done!" John shouts.

She stands up, wiping the soot off her knees, and grins. "I knew this day would come. Now, who is the real man amongst you? Is it going to be you, William? Or perhaps you will do this deed, Fred? Who is going to throw me in my furnace and be the hero with a lifetime of regret?"

She walks over to the furnace and opens the door. The heat wave blisters our faces from over ten feet away. Mary Lou stands off to the side as the heat tosses her hair around. She's still smiling as she asks, "Well? What are you waiting for, William? I'm right here."

Holding my arm in front of my face, I make my way over and pick her up in my arms. She kisses my cheek and seductively whispers, "Kill me now, and I'll live forever in what is mine!"

"Throw her in!" my companions yell.

I walk to the open door and my hand starts burning along with Mary's hair and dress. She's still grinning as I heave her into the furnace and laughs as I slam the door shut. Running over to the barrel of water, I stick my face and arms inside. We listen for her screams but hear nothing.

"Jesus Christ. Not a scream from her? Was she even human?" John asks.

"I don't know, but tonight this crematorium closes. We'll make it a house of love instead of one of pain." I reply, rubbing the soot off my face and arms.

June 1, 1954

I wipe my forehead, putting the last box down. This two-story brownstone is officially our new home. Out in the front yard, dusk shines a bright orange glow onto the house. Cindy walks towards me with a glass of water.

"My God, what a beautiful sight to see. I still can't believe we got this house so cheap from William Ross."

I wrap my arm around her waist and kiss her temple. "I believe they said the previous owner died, honey, but may god rest his soul. We are the luckiest people alive. Nowhere else in the world would we be able to afford a house built in 1848."

Cindy looks up at me and grins as the sun crouches down beneath the house. Darkness approaches. "We are. I can't wait until we have our house warming party. Everyone will enjoy themselves."

"Where are the boys? I haven't seen them at all since we got here?" I ask, puzzled.

Forgotten Past

"You know boys. They're probably exploring their new home."

"Yeah, you're probably right. Let's go inside and I'll try to figure out how to start that weird looking furnace."

We walk back inside, and I shout, "Tom! Billy! Come inside for dinner!"

I listen but there's no response. Cindy looks worried, so I yell even louder, "Tom! Billy! Get into the living room now!"

After a few minutes, Cindy shrugs her shoulders looking confused.

"Don't worry honey. We'll punish them when they get back. Where is the flashlight? I'll go light that furnace up," I say as she pulls open the box in the middle of the floor.

"Be careful, Jordan!"

"I will, don't worry."

I open the basement door and shine the light down the stairs. Slowly making my way down, the echo of each footstep cascades across my ears. I walk past numerous doors in the dank smelling basement and bat the cobwebs away. I see the furnace room ahead. The door creaks and whines as I open it to finally reveal a huge metal contraption.

"Don't touch that furnace…" A ghastly woman's voice whispers.

I turn around, petrified, trying to figure where the voice came from. I walk towards the door to see if Cindy is messing with me, but no one is there.

"Don't do it," the same voice whispers again.

I turn towards the furnace and open the main chamber, shining the light inside. There's a metal grate with a cement bottom.

"What the heck is this?" I think. *"It looks more like a baker's oven than a furnace. That explains why the chimney's so big."*

"Get away from there!" The voice calls out, louder this time.

I swing the flashlight around rapidly, and I hear Tom scream.

"Help us!"

I turn back to the furnace and see him inside. "What are you doing in there?" I ask.

"I'm stuck and can't get out," he responds.

I try to pull the grate out, but it's stuck. "Hang on, I'll come and get you out."

I crawl inside, making my way along the ten-foot grate, and grab Tom's arm. I shine the light and look into his soot covered face and discover a stranger. "You're not Tom," I whisper as the metal door slams shut.

"No, I'm not."

The boy disappears, and the smell of gas becomes overwhelming. I bang on the door with my flashlight as the face of a woman stares back at me.

"I told you to get away from my furnace."

"Who are you? What are you doing in my house?" I yell.

"You're in my house, and nobody touches what's mine!"

The gas keeps hissing as I start choking. There's an explosive sound behind me as flames engulf me. All I can see through the smoke is a glimpse of her smile.

October 12, 2004.

Sitting at the counter of Alison's coffee shop, I look at the new sign being placed above my business. "We Care Home Reality" I whisper, approvingly.

Three old men walk in and sit behind me. I listen as one of them asks, "You hear anything new on that old crematorium house? Or are those folks in office just giving the runaround about tearing it down?"

"Just a lot of hooey about the foundation being in great shape and nothing wrong with it," a second man answers.

"You're kidding. After what happened to that last family in 1954? You told them about Mary Lou Bell, right? My father told me how evil she was. I don't know how one woman could kill those children so mercilessly. That house needs to come down before another family meets their end," the third man grumbles.

The second man angrily responds,

"They just scoffed it off as me trying to embellish an old wives' tale. Yes, I've heard about her furnace of death. We need to do something, and soon," the second man replies.

"I'll try my hand at it this week," the first man joins back in. "They need to know that house kills people. My father and grandfather told me about Mary and her ways. It scared me from walking down old devil's road for a good chunk of my life. Never been so fearful of anything in my life."

"You and me both Edward. You remember Becky Anderson?"

"I do. My father used to say that those seven children, Becky included, were victims of Mary's rage. He used to say she was the devil incarnate and her soul was filled with despise and hate."

"Yes, and don't forget about that cursed furnace of hers. I was told that when she was thrown in she laughed at her executioners as she burnt to death," the first man continues.

"To this day those poor folks were never told anything, but I'm sure that's why they died in there."

"Check please!" I call out, leaving a ten on the counter. Alison walks over as I'm getting up to leave. "Keep the change," I state, walking to my car.

I get in and drive down old devil's road thinking, "This might just help my business get the start I need."

I stop in front of the for-sale sign and dial the number.

"Hello?" a man answers.

"Hi, I'm looking for Dean Cater?"

"Yes, that's me. I'm just in the middle of something. What can I do for you?"

"I'm calling about that house on old devil's road…"

"Yes, I know the house," he interrupts. "The people want forty-five thousand!"

"I have thirty if they're willing to go down to that," I reply anxiously.

"Yeah, done deal!"

"Great, I'll stop by your office within an hour," I hang up and turn the ignition again.

Getting out at Dean' office, I reach my hand out for a shake.

"I take it you have seen the house already? I'm sorry I didn't get your name," he greets me.

"I'm Gerald Kent, and yes I have. Can you tell me a bit of the background on this house?" I ask.

"I can, but I doubt you'll buy the house after hearing it."

"No, I'll buy the house regardless!"

"The last time that house was bought, the man slaughtered his entire family. Afterwards, he fired up the furnace in the basement, stepped right in, and closed the door on himself. That place has been emptied ever since. If you still want it, come inside. I have the papers all done up. How do you want to do this? Through a bank or have you got a check?"

"I have a check right here," I answer as we head inside.

"Last chance. Are you sure you want this house?"

"I'm sure. I have an idea for that house after I fix it up some."

July 6, 2018

"Now George. Remember what I told you. These people are really interested in this house, so make sure they buy it!"

"Yes, Mr. Kent," I reply. "But can I ask why it's been on the market so long?"

"Close the door."

After I get up and close the door, he continues.

"You don't repeat this to anyone, understand?"

"Yes sir."

"Back in 1954, a family of four moved in. I don't know who went nuts, but I believe the father did. He butchered his family in the basement, and I'm talking licking the funny farm from one end to the other nuts! He hung his boys on meat hooks in the freezer, and his wife was laying on an embalming table, completely drained of fluids. Now, the husband, this is why I say it was probably him… he literally turned the crematorium furnace on, went inside, and closed the door behind himself. Nuts, right?"

"Oh my God. You're serious, aren't you?" I reply, shocked as he nods.

"Ever since then, nobody's wants to buy the house. Today, you're going to sell that house to these out of towners."

"Yes, Mr. Kent."

"Don't worry, George, that was sixty-four years ago. We paid the local papers to remove any trace of that tragedy ever happening. Now all anyone knows is it used to be an old crematorium that was converted into a house. Don't worry, just tell them what you see, and let them decide for themselves if they like it or not. You've got this George."

He he points to the front door, so I get up and walk out of the room, trying to smile, to greet them. "Hello! I'm George Kaiser."

"Hi, George. This is my wife Cassie, our son Anthony, and I'm Alex Corson."

"Nice to meet you all. I'm guessing you'd like to take a look at the house?"

"Yes. We saw the picture on your website and fell in love with it immediately. Should we follow you there?" Mr. Corson replies.

"Sure, my car is the silver Buick beside your car. I'll be right out."

Mr. Kent waits for them to leave before coming over with the keys and papers to the house. "Sell this house," he whispers.

Getting into my car, I start it up head towards the wretched worn sign that reads old devil's road. I glance back every so often to see that they're still following. A short while later, we pull into the yard.

"Can we go take a look inside ourselves?" Mr. Corson asks, startling me.

"Absolutely," I answer, handing him the keys.

They dash towards the house and disappear inside. I wait outside, dwelling on what Mr. Kent said. Looking at the two-story building, I can't seem to comprehend what that father was thinking when he killed his family. Twenty minutes after they went in, the Corsons come out, still grinning ear to ear.

"We'll take it!" Mr. Corson happily shouts.

Taken aback, I quickly compose myself. "Sure! I brought the papers with me. Within a couple weeks, the house will be yours."

"This is the greatest house ever. You've made us the happiest family. Thank you!"

I grab the papers out of my car and point him through all of the signatures and initials. "You said two weeks the latest?"

"Yes, it should be no more than two weeks before this house is yours," I answer. "I'll call you as soon as everything is ready for you to take procession."

He nods before joining his family and driving away.

Driving back to the office, what Mr. Kent said still plays in my mind. When I get there, Mr. Kent looks like a drooling puppy in the window as he watches me.

"Well? Did they buy it?" He asks when I'm finally inside and at my desk.

"Yes, they bought the house." I answer snappy, a sense of guilt gnawing at me.

"Hot damn! George, you have earned my respect."

"Sir, I have to ask. That story you told me earlier… was that to mess with me?"

"Hell no. Every word is as true as the day I was born. Why? Did you say something to them?"

"No, I was just trying to go over what happened to that family in my head."

"Don't worry about it. That was over sixty years ago. Besides, they cleaned the remains out of there. I'll deal with these, and tomorrow I'll cut you a check. Now, don't worry about this house any more. You sold it for a quarter of a million dollars. That's huge considering nobody has showed any interest in it before. You did fine work, and you gave them a happy home. Take the rest of the day off. You look like you need the time to relax."

"Yes, Mr. Kent," I answer. I walk out the door and get into my car. I sit there, staring at myself in the mirror, feeling like I did something wrong. I drive down old devil road and stop in front of the house. As I get out and walk into the large yard, a soft breeze caresses my face.

"Hey! What are you doing here?" A man's voice shouts angrily.

I jump, startled, and turn around to see an old man standing behind me. He comes down the driveway with a menacing look on his face and stops in front of me as he glares at the house.

"Don't suppose you're one of them people who sold this house?" he asks.

"I am. Just sold it this afternoon," I answer, as his glare turns to me.

"Damn fool. That there's the house of death. Only fools condemn unknowing folks to this house. My pop used to work for the woman who owned this place when it was the Crematorium, back when I was a child. He told me tales that would give me nightmares for weeks. Said she once threw her husband in that oven and baked his squirrel ass. Most folks around here stayed away or moved if she looked at them the wrong way. Now you've gone and sold this place. Don't you live around here?"

"No, I actually live one town over. Why? What's wrong with this house?" I ask.

"What gives you the right to sell what you know nothing about. When this cremation was built, the man who originally owned it died in the late 1880's. He was cursed from the get go. Everyone that came after died, some within months of owning it. That is, until Mary-Lou

Bell. She was the devil's spawn according to my pop. She put as many living folks through that furnace as dead folks. You'd best not owe her a dime when payment was due, or she'd take your child and get that dime from their blood."

"You're kidding, right? No one would be that vicious," I state, frightened.

"Our neighbor at the time, Ralph Anderson, had his wife Olivia cremated and his crops hadn't come off when he owed her the last $12.37. Mary came in and snatched his daughter, gave him an hour to pay. Sadly, it was a bad time for everyone. None of us could help him. Mary threw that child in there as if she'd been dead a week and burned her up."

"Dear God... she did that?" I gasp, appalled.

"That and worse. She's the kind of woman who was hired by lowlifes and they paid her well. Tell those people this place isn't for sale lest you be creating more holes for people to be buried in."

"I'll talk to my boss in the morning and get him to tear that contract up," I answer.

"No, you won't. You're like all the other times. I've watched folks come n go in body bags and this won't be different. Mary owns this place and she'll never let her home go."

"Excuse me? All the others? What do you mean by that?"

"Boy, you're dumber than a bag of hammers. This house been sold more times than Old Joe's fifty-year-old tractor. Every year someone new buys the place and dies in there," he states before turning to walk away.

"Hey! I just listened to you berate me for the past five minutes. I deserve an apology!" I shout after him.

"An apology? For what? You being dumb? I'm not the one making graves for good people."

July 20, 2018.

I sit, waiting for Mr. Kent to come in, looking at my watch. I'm hoping I can try to convince him not to sell to the Corsons. Almost trembling with fear, my leg bounces rapidly. I see Mr. Kent's Mercedes pull up and watch him get out and come in the door.

"Not today, George. The sale is final and that is all I want to hear."

"But sir, you lied! That house has been sold every year."

"Look here, George. If you have a problem working here, you can be replaced. We are salesmen. So what if I lied? I built my house selling that house hundreds of times. If your conscious is eating away at you this bad, there's the door."

"I quit!" I yell, turning and walking out as Mr. Kent shouts and stands up grabbing my arm,

"Look here, you ungrateful shit. I gave you a job and you said you'd do anything to make my kind of money. Well, this is how I make my money. I sell dreams. So what if people die? Everyone dies. If I didn't sell this house every chance I get, I'd be out of business by now. Nobody buys any of the other houses we have for sale, just that one."

"How many people have died there?"

"I don't know, maybe a thousand. Give or take a few."

"Jesus Christ. A thousand? Are you kidding? I'm sorry, Mr. Kent. I may have said that I would do anything for your kind of money, but I'm not going to go along with this scheme of yours."

I see his fist as he punches me in the face and I hit the floor. He sits on my chest, and after a few more punches he grabs my face. "Look here, George. I have a great business, and I'm not going to let you ruin it because you feel bad for a few dead people. You and I are going to take a drive."

He punches me in the face again and everything fades to black.

I open my eyes and try to move, but I'm tied up. "What's going on?" I mutter, feeling woozy.

"Hello, George. I thought you might have wanted to stay asleep for this, but I guess not?"

"What are you doing?"

"Your services are no longer needed at We Care Home Reality. I figured I'd fire you properly and keep my sugar home making me money. I bought this house fourteen years ago for $30,000, so other than your commission, every dime belongs to me."

"Oh my God, you're a madman!"

"No, I'm a smart man who makes tons of money. I have to get going but enjoy your short-term unemployment."

He slams the metal door shut, and I smell gas. I scream but the hissing sound only gets louder.

Crematorium house.

"Stupid man," I mutter, watching though the peephole as the flames devour George. "Shit, this is going to be close. They're coming in an hour. Hurry up and burn already, George."

Forgotten Past

I wait half an hour before turning the gas off and open the door with gloves on. Seeing George's charred remains, I grab the rake and drag his bones towards me, placing them in a nearby metal container.

Getting back to the office, Mr. Corson and his wife are already waiting by the door. "I'm sorry, but George couldn't be here," I say, running towards them. "He decided to play Houdini. He just went up in smoke and disappeared."

"No worries, we're just excited to get into our new house."

"I'm excited, too. I can't wait until you send me pictures of what you've done to the place."

"Do you have the papers?" Mr. Corson asks.

"Yes, please come in. I'll get you the keys as well."

I quickly make my way to my office, grab the file off my desk, and walk back to them. "Alright, here's the keys to your new home. Here are all your papers. Signed, sealed, and delivered."

"I can't thank you enough. We've wanted a house like this for years."

I hold my hands up, "no, thank you for taking the old girl off my hands. I am the one who is truly grateful. I hope you don't mind if I stop by here and there to make sure you're still enjoying it?"

"Not at all! Perhaps we'll have you over for supper one of these days."

"I would love to, but if you're going to, let's make it no sooner than say next week? That'll let you settle in nicely."

"You can bet on it. Thank you again, Mr. Kent."

"That's what I'm here for. I know you'll enjoy that house. I have some work to finish, but I'll visit you soon." I reply, as we shake hands.

They hurry out to their car and disappear. Walking into my office, laughing, I wonder how long it'll be before my house is back on the market. Sitting down, I open the drawer and take out a thick folder. It makes a dull thud as I drop it on my desk. Opening it, I glance through the pages upon pages of owners who have passed on in my house.

The phone rings, taking mem out of my thoughts. I answer it, "Hello, We Care Home Reality. Mr. Kent speaking."

"Hi, I was checking your website. You have two-story listed for sale?" a man's voice inquires.

"Yes, I do. Are you interested in viewing it?"

"Yes, and the sooner the better."

"Let me see my schedule here… Yes, I can probably fit you in next week. How does Tuesday sound?"

"Can you make sure you let me know if anyone else is interested in it? My wife and I are looking to start a family and this house is perfect!"

"Congratulations on starting a family. I'll hold this house for you even if I have to stay closed until you arrive. Can I have your name and number please?"

"Christopher Chad, and my number is 555-9687. I greatly appreciate this. I'll talk to you on Tuesday!"

"That sounds great. I'll talk to you soon, Mr. Chad, and thank you for calling." I reply, hanging up the phone. I grab the folder and kiss it. "Thank you!"

July 23, 2018.

I pull into the driveway and park behind Mr. Corson's car, get out, and take my shades off. Walking up to the door, I knock before grabbing my key from my pocket and unlocking the door. I head to the wall between the kitchen and hallway, looking around cautiously, and open the secret panel that returns power to the lights downstairs.

"What a blessing you've been since I installed you," I say, patting the wall and closing the panel. I head downstairs and a familiar odor wafts past me. I open each door as I make my way down the hall and whisper, "where are you? Mr. and Mrs. Corson? Hello?"

I open another door. "Ah, there's your beautiful wife, Mr. Corson!" I state, looking at her disemboweled body on the embalming table. "It's a shame. Oh well, more dollars coming my way tomorrow."

I take off my jacket and put on an old apron to carry the pieces of Mrs. Corson to the furnace room. Opening the door, I throw her remains inside. After opening several other doors, I finally find their son cowering in in a corner.

"Mom and dad are dead!" He cries.

"Yes, they are. How come you're not?" I ask, curiously.

"I hid in here. There's a ghost woman who killed them."

"I see. Well, this presents a small problem for me. A ghost woman, hey? Come with me and you can show me what that mean old ghost did. Don't worry, I won't let her hurt you. It's Anthony, right?" I ask, as he nods.

He shuffles towards me, looking around scared. I hold out my hand as he grabs it.

"Now, show me what happened to your dad," I say, as we walk together.

"I came downstairs with my dad to light the furnace. He said there was something inside, so he went inside to get it out. As soon as he went in, a woman appeared and slammed the door shut. Dad was screaming as she turned that knob. I tried to open the door, but she threw me into the corner. I heard an explosion and dad was screaming even louder. That's when I ran into that room to hide."

I can see him crying but continue. "I see. Was the door open like this? And your dad all the way inside? Can you show me?"

He walks closer and lets out a scream when he sees his mom. I snatch him up and throw him inside, slamming the door shut.

"You're losing your touch, lady!" I yell, turning the gas on and igniting the furnace.

Anthony's screams fade away. As the furnace burns, I walk around and remove the family's personal items from around the house in preparation for Mr. Chad, staging the house to look as if people are moving out.

After six hours, I head back to the basement to make sure the bones are dust. Once everything is cleaned, I reopen the panel upstairs and shut off the basement's electricity.

Leaving the home, I run into an old man standing at the edge of the driveway. I wave to him but he glares as he walks down the driveway.

"Where's that other one?" he asks.

"Excuse me? Oh. You mean George?"

"Yea, he's none too bright. Sold this house of death to them unknowing folks."

"I guess. Who are you?" I ask.

"Vern Demister. I live down the road. I tried to get the dimwit to reconsider selling to them folks."

I cross my arms as I nod. "Oh, that was you who was trying to interfere with the sale. Yes, I had to fire him. Might I ask what your problem with this house is?"

"This is the house of death. No one should ever be here."

"First of all, I'm shocked at this revelation. I'll make sure nobody else buys this house again if it's really the house of death. Thank you, but I must get going. I have a thousand things to do. Pleasure meeting you!"

I watch as he turns to leave, get in my car, and stare at him in the mirror. I put it in reverse and slam the gas pedal to the floor. He turns just in time to see me, but not in time to move. Stopping the engine, I get out to check on him.

"I'm sorry, Vern. Let me get you some help," I say, looking around to make sure nobody saw what happened.

"Please stop, that hurts," he whispers as I drag him into the house.

"Yes, I bet. It hurts me, too. George was a good one, but after what you did? Sheesh! I'll make sure to keep your secret. Nobody will ever know what you said about this house again."

I flick on the power before dragging him down the basement stairs.

"Come on, let's get you warmed up."

July 24, 2018.

I keep an eye on the clock, waiting for Mr. Chad and his wife to come check out the house. I glance out the window and see the sheriff coming towards the door. He opens it and walks in.

"Hey Mr. Kent, how's business?"

"Hey Todd. You know, slow. I have a possible buyer for the old Bell home. They're supposed to be coming in today," I answer.

"How long have you been trying to sell that house now? A few years or more?"

"Business isn't what it used to be."

"I'll get down to the brass tacks of why I'm here. I got a call from George Kaiser's girlfriend. She said he never showed up at home yesterday."

"Really? I had to fire him yesterday. It's too bad, he was a hard worker. I gave him a great farewell bonus."

"She said you two were arguing over the Bell house. He didn't want to sell it because of a story you told him?" he continues, looking at me closely.

"Yes, he lost the sale of the house. I won't deny I was mad. We argued for a while, and that's when I told him he could keep the check I cut for him. That's the last I saw of him before happily walked out the door."

"Now Gerald, I know you just didn't let him off that easy. Tell me what really happened."

"I'm serious, Todd. He left right out that door, no questions asked. I swear I didn't touch him. The phone rang before I could. I answered the call while he left."

"I guess I'm going to have to go with that. I'll tell Chrissy that George probably went on a road trip for a new job. I'll talk to you soon Gerald."

"Yes, tell her he'll probably be back in a day or two. You're welcome here anytime, Todd," I answer, watching as he makes his way to the door.

He stops as he turns the handle, "By the way, what story did you tell him that had him scared to sell the old house?"

"You remember that old tale about the town gathering to get revenge on Mary Lou for cremating all those people by throwing her in the furnace? That one."

"Jesus Gerald. You know we've been trying to bury that secret since 1938. Shit, no wonder the boy sped out of here so fast."

"Oh well. It looks like my possible buyer is here, Todd," I reply, looking out the window.

"Alright, just don't tell him that story. Christ!"

"I won't, lesson learned. See you later, Todd."

He walks out as a young couple walks in.

"Mr. Kent, I presume?" the man addresses me.

"Yes, that's me. You must be Christopher," I answer, holding out my hand.

"Yes, and this is my wife Tiffany."

"Pleasure to meet you both. I'm guessing you'd like to see the house?"

"Yes, please, if we could. You had the asking price at a quarter of a million. Would you come down to two if we like it?"

I stare at them both for a moment. "I never do this, but if you really like it I think I can persuade the seller to let it go. After all, I'm about making dreams come true," I reply.

"Wow, thank you!"

"No, thank you! Come on, I'll show you your new home," I say as we head out the door.

They make their way to their car as I hop in mine and holler, "Follow me, it's a little bumpy." They nod as I get ready to drive and we head down Old Devil's road. We pull into the driveway an Tiffany jumps out of the car, excited.

"I love it! It has so much character."

I pull the keys out of my pocket and jingle them causing Christopher to turn and smile. He grabs the keys and they head inside as I follow behind them. As they check out the house, I stand in the living room looking at the boxes.

"You touched my furnace," a ghastly woman's voice whispers.

I run outside, frightened, and turn around to see a ghostly woman standing at the door with her hair in a bun. She glares at me hard as I hold onto my chest. She vanishes shortly after, and Chad and Tiffany come walking out.

"What happened? We saw you running out of the house."

"I had to take a call, but my cell phone won't work inside. I missed the call, so I'll call them back," I answer, trying to laugh.

"Alright, we'll take it," Chad says.

"Great! I'll start on the paperwork right away. When did you want to move in?"

"Right away. I know there are boxes in there, but if we give them a few days to move do you think that would work?"

"Well, according to the owner, they left everything they didn't want behind. You can consider it a gift from the owner."

"Really? We can move in right away?"

"Well, first you'd need the money, and then you are free to move in," I answer.

"My father is buying it for us. We should have the money tomorrow."

"Really, that soon? Then sure! We'll sign the papers and you can move in right away," I replay as they kiss each other.

July 28, 2018.

I'm sitting in my office, filing another couple away, when I see the sheriff come in. I quickly shut the drawer as he walks into my office, an angry look on his face. "What's up today, Todd?" I ask.

"We seem to have a problem, Gerald. George still hasn't come home, and now Vern Demister is missing too. You remember him, don't you? He's 106 years old. Seems a lot of missing people are coming up lately, and according to his neighbor Frank he was coming to talk to you about selling that house. I questioned him more on that issue and seems that people are always coming and going from there. Why would Frank be telling me people are always there? Didn't you tell me you just sold the house?"

"Selling the house constantly? Are you sure he isn't crazy, Todd? I sold the house a couple days ago," I reply, trying not to lose my cool.

"One of my deputies checked your website, and found that quite a few missing persons match up with the people who answered your web ad. I called some of the people myself, and according to their banks and accounts it seems these people spent a quarter of a million on that house. Your asking price. You're telling me all these people vanished into thin air? I have to ask myself how someone would spend hundreds of thousands of dollars on a house, and then up and vanish."

"Now look, Todd. You and I both know I would never pull a scam like what you're trying to say."

"Cut the crap, Gerald!" he yells. "I know what you're up to, and once I have the evidence I need, you'll be in jail. I knew you were dirty, but this is downright disgraceful."

"Honest, Todd. I have every record. Give me two weeks to get them from my accountant, and I'll bring you every bit of proof, I swear."

"Two weeks? Alright, I'll give you two weeks. Or until my deputies find what we need. Don't leave town. I don't like chasing people, but I will if I have to."

Todd turns and starts walking out but turns one more time. "I'll see you in two weeks, but remember, I'll be watching you."

The phone rings as he stalks out. I pick it up and answer nervously. "Hello?"

"Hi!" the voice on the line exclaims. "My name is Isabelle. I noticed you have a fabulous 1800's house for sale. Is it still available?"

"Yes, it is available. When would you like to see it?"

"Is today possible? This house is just what I'm looking for."

"I'm located on Main Street, We Care Home Reality," I reply.

"Perfect! See you in a little bit, Mr. Kent."

I hang up and grab another buyer's form. I fill it out quickly and barely finish before a twenty-something girl in a red dress with brown hair in a bun walks in. She smiles and saunters over to me. I can't help but think she looks familiar but can't place it.

"Mr. Kent?" she asks softly.

"You must be Isabelle. It's a pleasure to meet you," I reply, shaking her hand.

"I'm sure. Now, let's get these pesky forms out of the way. I want that lovely house and I want it now!"

"Sight unseen? This is a first for me," I reply, handing her the form as she passes me a check. "Can I ask why the rush?"

"I saw the house and just had to have it. Of course, I figured someone bought it already, but I'm glad to be wrong. A woman always knows what she wants, and I want that house."

"I'll get the keys for you," I reply, walking to my desk. I hold them out to her with the papers.

"Thank you! I'll be on my way now."

"I'll come by and check on you in a day or two to make sure you're satisfied," I reply.

"That would be most kind. Thank you again."

"I'll see you later, Isabelle," I reply as she saunters out.

I look at the check with a grin and whisper, "Yes, untraceable currency. I must make plans to take a vacation in a tropical Island. After I dispose of Isabelle's body, of course."

July 31, 2018.

"Yes, I want to transfer all my accounts. I'll have the new account set up by then. Yes. Okay, bye!" I say, hanging up the phone. Everything is set. All that's left is to go and dispose of Isabelle. I would have loved to get with her first, but money talks and sex can be bought. I close up and walk out to my car, get in, and drive down Old Devil Road. I see her car parked in the driveway and get out with my spare key in hand. Opening the door, I walk over to the wall and turn the electricity back on.

Walking down the stairs, I whisper, "Isabelle? Where are you my dear?" I open door after door, glancing in each room, but find nothing. I check around for any signs of her body, and even check the furnace, but it's clean. "What the heck?" I shout, confused.

"You touched my furnace again," a woman's voice calls out.

I run out the door and back up the stairs, nearly running into Isabelle. "Oh, thank God! I thought something happened to you," I say, trying to catch my breath.

"What did you think happened to me, Mr. Kent?" she looks worried, as she stands there holding a cup of something.

"Someone said they heard a scream from the house. I raced down here to make sure you were okay," I respond.

"That is kind of you, but it wasn't me who screamed. I have no reason to scream."

"I'm just glad you are safe," I answer, taking a deep breath and closing the door to the basement. "I probably should be going now."

"Stay. I wouldn't be a good host if I didn't offer to make us a snack. After all, you came all this way for me."

"Sure, that would be great," I reply, caught in her smile.

"Would you like some tea? It's a special blend of my great-great grandma's recipe?"

"I would love some," I answer, sitting down. I can't help but wonder how she isn't she dead like all the others. She gracefully moves across the floor and comes back with a cup of what looks like green tea. She pours it gently as she sits next to me.

"Who told you I screamed?" she asks. She sits in the chair looking like a model as she looks at me, puzzled.

"One of the farmers down the road. I guess he was playing with me," I reply, shaking my head.

She leans forward as I take a sip of the boiling tea. "Yeah, that's terrible that people do that. They should be punished. I hope you weren't in the middle of anything too important?"

"No, just the same old boring paperwork that is my life," I reply, feeling funny as I shake my head.

"Are you okay, Mr. Kent?"

"Huh…? Oh, yeah. This must be some tea your grandma made," I reply, feeling lightheaded. I watch as Isabelle become distorted and fuzzy.

"Mr. Kent? You okay? You seem to be drooling. Mr. Kent…?"

Her voice fades as everything goes darker.

Crematorium house.

Wake up, sleepy head," I whisper, tapping Mr. Kent on the cheek with two fingers. I watch as his eyes slowly open as he tries to focus on me. I smile.

"What happened to me?" he slurs.

"You decided to fall asleep after my great-great grandma's tea," I answer, watching him look around.

"Am I in the basement?" he asks.

"Yes, where else would you expect to be?"

"Get me out of here, please. It's not safe down here," he starts to panic, noticing he's strapped to the table.

"Let me tell you a story first," I grin. "My mother showed me pictures of this place when I was younger. Mary Lou Bell was my grandma. I figured what better way to honor her than me living in the same house she did."

"She didn't have any family," he interrupts.

I cover his mouth. "Yes, she did. But when she started dealing with the lowlifes at the time, she changed my great grandmother's name to Ramses to keep her safe if anything went south. Great grandma Mary Lou, she was a badass lady. I only hope to be as great as she was. Truthfully, I've been watching you use my great-great grandmother's house to make millions of dollars for yourself. Now tell me, isn't that a tad bit greedy?" I state.

"Do you want the money? I'll give you all the money if you want."

"No, I don't want anything like that, Mr. Kent. I just want my great-great grandma's house. She wants you, though. You have been making her angry using her furnace for your greed. I guess she has been waiting years for you, but you keep flipping that switch upstairs. I've got to run now, but don't worry. I'm make sure to flip the switch on my way out. Thanks again, Mr. Kent, I love this house. I'd say I'll talk with you after, but I have a feeling you won't be here when I get back."

"No, please! I don't deserve this!" he calls out.

I stop and turn around. "Mr. Kent, lying to a lady? Those words will see you burn in hell. Or the furnace. Either way, you'll burn. I have to go now, but my grandma will keep you company. And remember, it's not nice to yell in someone else's house," I reply, politely, as he continues to scream.

I stop at the top of the stairs and shout down, "I'm borrowing your car. I'll leave it behind your business."

"Get me out of here!" he screams back.

I open the wall and turn off the electricity, listening as his screams grow louder as I leave. I place some plastic over the driver's side of his car, put on my gloves, and get in. I drive into town and park behind Mr. Kent's business, roll the plastic up, and placing it in the recycle bin. Walking over to Alison's coffee shop across the street, I sit down at the counter.

"What can I get you Miss?" the waitress asks me.

"Do you have tea?"

"Yes, we do. What flavor would you like?"

"Perhaps green tea. It reminds me of my grandmother," I reply.

"My grandmother enjoyed green tea as well. I'll be right back."

"Thank you!"

The door opens and a police officer walks in and looks at me strangely before coming closer.

"Are you passing through ma'am?" he asks.

"No, I actually just moved into the brownstone on Old Devil's Road."

"He sold it again?"

"I'm sorry? I bought that house outright!" I reply.

"No, I'm sorry," he looks embarrassed and answers apologetically. "I meant he kills the people who buy the house, so he can resell it again."

"Oh dear, really? He seemed to have a real fire under his behind when he sold it to me," I respond.

"What do you mean fire under his ass?"

"I gave him a cashier's check and he seemed quick to want to be gone. He had the papers signed by the time I arrived. He gave me the keys a few days ago and that was the last I saw of Mr. Kent."

"I knew I shouldn't have trusted him. He's probably left town! I'm sorry, I have to go. Nice meeting you miss…?"

"Isabelle Bell," I reply.

"Nice to meet you Miss Bell. I hope you enjoy our hospitality."

"I hope you get Mr. Kent, especially if he did those horrible things to others," I answer disgusted.

"Yes ma'am, we will get him one way or another."

I watch him run out the door and across the street as the waitress comes back.

"Did I hear you right? You bought the old crematorium house?" she asks.

"Yes, it's such a beautiful house," I answer.

"Yes, but such a horrible history."

"I know my great-great grandma made life miserable for a lot of people, but she sure empowered women of the time," I respond.

"That she did. You're Mary Lou Bell's great granddaughter?"

"I am, but don't worry. I'm not going to take people to the furnace."

"I am glad to hear that. I think you'll fit in here just fine. The tea is on me."

"Thank you. Perhaps one of these days you can come over and the tea will be on me." I reply, smiling.

Synopsis

Mr. Gerald Kent found money was all he needed to be happy. Making his dreams come true, he sells a home over and over again. Mary Lou Bell, a woman who murdered those that owed her money, owned this home. Mr. Kent loves money more than life itself, and it's put to the test when Mary Lou's granddaughter Isabelle Smith (Bell) moves into the house. This time, Mr. Kent's money-making scheme is in jeopardy.

Pankratz

The Sanatorium

Pankratz

During the rise of tuberculous, or the White Death, in the early twentieth century in Saskatchewan, the lung association along with the government of Saskatchewan and the city of Saskatoon began drafting plans to build a hospital to house the affected by 1923. These plans became a reality in 1925 when the doors to the Sanatorium opened. The early methods of treating tuberculous were barbaric to say the least, but as years progressed, so did the methods of treating patients. The years between the opening and closing of the Sanatorium are sketchy at best. Everyone has a story, and no two stories are the same. One thing does remain consistent though, and that's fear. Fear of hospitals. Just being in one can send a person into a panic attack.

In 2001, I met a man with this fear. This wasn't a horror movie fear; his fear was real. Up until that moment, I had never met anyone who would go as pale as he did when the door to his hospital room closed. Asking him about this reaction, he began telling me his story. A horror story I have never forgotten to this day. Sadly, he never finished telling his story as he passed away from cancer of the blood a few days after I began talking with him. Not being able to complete our talk, I was left with so many gaps that creating a complete story was impossible. This story is fictional as most of what he told me can't be, or won't be, verified by others.

Today, the Sanatorium building has been gone for 29 years and only the Bowerman house remains as a testament of what once stood about one hundred feet away. The building may be lost, but the ghost stories flourish. This story is based on what I was told, what I have heard, and what I have seen with my own eyes.

Sitting listening to the radio with my arm around Janet, we stare at the old Sanatorium as dusk turns to night. We stare at the outline of the building as it slowly disappears into the darkness. "Janet," I whisper in her ear. "Let's go check out that old hospital."

"That's where you want to take me? Are you kidding me, Jeff?" she replies.

I look into her eyes and see she's mad. I touch her cheek with the back of my hand and answer, "Yes, it will be quiet and we won't be disturbed."

"Why don't we go back to your house? This place gives me the creeps."

"Oh, come on, it will be fun," I whisper, twisting my fingers in her curly brown hair. "How is it going to be fun, Jeff?" she asks, starting to sound annoyed.

"It just will be. Trust me, Janet."

"Okay, fine. Let's go then. Next time we go where I want to go."

I continue to kiss her, and our lips meet. After a few minutes of passion, I get out of my car and walk around to the trunk. I grab a couple of flashlights and an old checkered blanket, handing a flashlight to Janet as I slam the trunk closed. The Sanatorium is barely visible in the darkness.

"This place is creeping me out. Let's just go," Janet says, shining her flashlight around.

"Aw come on. We're here now...let's check it out," I reply trying to make Janet smile. "How did you find this place anyway?"

"Sam. He mentioned he brought his girl here. According to him, it was the best sex they ever had."

"Sam? Sam is an idiot. He's always cheating on Ruby with other girls."

"I know, but he knows where the good spots are. Let's have some fun."

We walk down the long road towards the building. The darkness makes it blend in with the night and the sounds are eerie enough to make anyone jump out of their skin. As I shine my flashlight in front of me, I find a spot behind the building. I place the blanket down as Janet shines her light all around. Sitting down, I grab Janet gently.

"I get the feeling someone is watching us," she whispers.

"Don't worry, Janet. Who would be here anyway?" I coax her down onto the blanket and place my lips on hers. Shortly after unbuttoning her shirt, noises begin creeping in around us. Grabbing my flashlight, a little frightened myself, I shine it all over the place. Janet grabs her flashlight and does the same thing.

"Jeff... let's just go. Please?"

"Come on, baby, you're just spooked. Nobody has been here for eight years. Besides, you have me worked up," I reply, putting my flashlight down.

"Someone's out there, Jeff... please, let's just go."

"I'm here. Don't worry, I'll protect you," I respond, helping her back down. We kiss again but are interrupted by a loud bang.

"What was that?" Janet shrieks.

Sitting up, I grab the flashlight and walk around shouting, "Come out, you chicken!" I walk towards a set of trees making but see nothing but grass.

"I don't see anything Janet... Janet?" I turn around, but she's not there. I hear a door slam and see a beam of light inside the building's broken window.

"Come inside," a ghastly voice whispers.

Walking inside, I listen for any noises. There's dripping water, and another bang in the distance. Shining my light from left to right down the hall, I stop at every doorway, knowing she must be close by. I only see abandoned beds and trays.

"Janet!" I shout, as her name echoes. I walk to the end of the hall and open the door slowly, still listening for any sounds at all. "Come on, Janet. Enough is enough already, you win. We'll go somewhere else," I shout, but still nothing. Heading up the stairs, I hear a muffled scream at the other end of the hallway.

"Janet, is that you? Where are you?" I scream, running to the second floor. My voice echoes down the hall and fades once more. Walking slowly, I move the flashlight back and forth.

"Help!" a heart-stopping scream calls out from the other end of the hall.

Running as fast as I can, I slip just as I reach the doorway, hitting my head on the wall and floor as I fall. The flashlight flies out of my hand and smashes. Grabbing my head, I sit up and feel around for the light. Hearing Janet scream again, I bolt up only to trip over the debris.

Inside the room, I feel my way around in the dark. My hands touch something metal and something wet. "Janet?"

"Shh!" a ghastly man's voice whispers.

"Who are you?" I yell as I move around, slipping on something wet on the floor. I bang my head but keep moving. Feeling around on the floor, I crawl closer to the dripping sound. I reach my hand up until I touch something warm. "Janet?" I feel around until I get to the top of her head. "Janet, where's all your hair? What is this?" I start to shout.

"She needed surgery to correct her illness, and so do you," the man's voice returns.

"Who the hell are you?" I shout, trying to stand up and slipping.

"Dr. Steven Delve. You need help."

"What did you do to Janet?" I scream, seeing two red eyes peering at me.

"I saved her just like I am going to save you."

"Stay away from me!" I shout as the eyes move closer.

"There is no place to run. Just lay down."

Something picks me up and throws me against the wall where I land on a bed. I feel a hand around my neck.

"Good boy, you'll feel better soon."

A sharp burning pain in my ribs makes me scream and breathing becomes difficult.

"You'll feel better soon. Now, let's see what's going on in your head."

I feel a sharp burning pain in my forehead as everything goes blank.

Bedford Road Collegiate

I wonder where Janet is. She's supposed to meet me here to get our papers for history back. I haven't seen her for two days now and I'm starting to get worried. Glancing over at Sam, I think out loud, "I wonder where Janet and Jeff are. They haven't been at the school for a few days."

"Yeah, I haven't seen them since I told Jeff to take Janet to the old Sanatorium. I said it was the best place to get laid," he laughs.

"What? You are an ass, Sam! Why would you do that?" "To see if he would! Don't get your hair in a knot, they're probably having a great time."

"That place is haunted!"

"So what? A little scare will do Jeff some good."

"I used to live by there. That place is haunted. My grandmother used to tell us about what would happen there. She said when it opened in 1935 hundreds of people with tuberculous were patients there. There were so many people coming in and they had to find doctors. I guess there was one doctor who went mad trying to find a cure. He killed patients in the process. Grandma says he is condemned to stay there forever."

"I think your grandma smoked too much weed," Sam chuckles.

"You are an idiot! Everyone knows old people know things. My grandma isn't into telling lies," I shout as people stop and stare.

"Everyone tells lies. Even my grandma tell lies."

"Why would my grandma lie about that place?" I ask, shaking my head.

"Why does anyone lie? To make it more interesting."

"My grandma isn't like that, but let's check it out then. Unless you're afraid?"

"I'm not scared of anything."

"Good. We'll go right after school," I reply.

"I'll meet you in the parking lot."

After school, I walk down the hall towards the door to see if Sam is still there. He's standing by his car trying to look cool with his arms crossed. I walk over to him and ask, "You ready?"

"Bring it on, Amy."

Getting in, Sam peels out of the parking lot. He parks on the street of the Sanatorium and we walk through the open gate. There's another car parked a way down the road.

"Isn't that Jeff's car?" I ask.

"Yeah, but he would never leave his car parked here for so long. They must still be here, Amy."

"Hopefully, they didn't get hurt in the building," I respond, with an uneasy feeling in my stomach.

"Well, let's hurry up and get in there."

I run as fast as I can, trying to keep up to Sam as he sprints towards the building. The front door is padlocked so we head around to the back. I see a messed up checkered blanket by some trees and instantly recognize it. "Look at that blanket. They must have been out here," I shout to Sam who's already at the door.

"Yeah, and this door is open. Let's see if we can find them inside."

"Jedd? Janet?"

We walk down the hall looking in every room. My footsteps echo loudly down the halls.

"Look, two sets footprints," Sam interrupts my thoughts, pointing to the ground.

We follow them to the end of the hall and up the half-darkened stairway. The echoes of our footsteps are as loud as can be.

Stopping at the top of the stairs, we look around and see signs of activity everywhere. There are traces of blood on the wall and floors.

I pick up two pieces of a flashlight and reassemble it. I try to turn it on but it's broken.

"I think those are Jeff's handprints," Sam says, examining the wall.

"Maybe they went into that room," I say, pointing to the nearby room.

Sam slowly walks in as I follow behind, noticing an awful smell. "Oh my word. That smell is awful," I gag, covering my nose.

"Yeah, no kidding, I can't make out what it is?"

"It almost smells like something rotting?"

"What was this place used for, Amy?"

"I don't know. My grandma said people with tuberculous were held here, and they tried to help them," I answer, looking around at the old beds, dirty and covered with leaves.

"Why did it close?"

"It wasn't needed anymore. I think that was in 1978."

"I'd say by the smell that it's open again."

"Yeah, there's no way a scent like that would carry on…"

"That bed is bloodstained," Sam cuts me off.

"You don't think Jeff did anything to Janet do you, Sam?" I reply, horrified at the sight.

"No. I don't think Jeff has the balls to do anything like that."

Walking around the room, the smell is overpowering. I pick up another flashlight and this one works.

"Look at the wall above the bed," I say, illuminating it with the beam. "Holy shit. Did Jeff throw Janet against the wall Sam?"

"That's definitely someone's body imprint. Maybe Jeff did do something to Janet?"

"That blood is probably Janet's. We have to tell the police what happened here," I panic.

"I can't believe Jeff would do something like that."

As I stand looking at the blood-soaked bed, tears flow. "Poor Janet. Let's get out of here," I sniffle.

We run back to Sam's car and race to the nearest pay phone to call the police. We drive back to the sanatorium to meet the officers when they arrive.

"You two, what are your names?" the officer abruptly demands.

"I'm Sam Elroy, and this is Amy Cruz," Sam responds for us.

"Amy, you said on the phone that your friends were in here dead?" the officer says, while writing down our names.

"No, I said by the looks of what we could see, something happened to them. The smell in the last room on the second floor is appalling. It smells like something is rotting," I answer, as he jots down what I'm saying.

"We checked everywhere, but the basement because it's too dangerous to go down those steps. There are no dead bodies in there. What I think is your friends got carried away with whatever they were doing and left."

I stare at him confused. The blood on the bed. There's no way it could be anything else but murder.

"Listen, officer. My friend's car is parked over there. He would never leave his car alone. Something bad happened to them," Sam yells.

"Look, Sam. Amy. We checked the whole place out. There are no bodies in there. I suggest you go home and forget about it. If anything happens, we have your contact information and will get in touch with you. Okay?"

Seeing the officer getting mad, I quickly reply, "Yes, officer," before grabbing Sam's arm and walking back to the car. We get in, not saying a word, and sit as the anger on Sam's face growing. He drives to my house but stares straight ahead.

"That cop was full of shit," he finally breaks the silence. "You and I both know something happened there."

"I know. I bet the cops found those bodies and just aren't saying so."

"I get that feeling too, Amy. Let's go there tomorrow and see what we can find?"

"I can't tomorrow, but the day after I can," I answer.

"After school again?"

"Yeah, that works for me."

I get out and he waves before driving off.

Heading inside, my mom calls, "Amy, is that you?"

"Yes, mom." I yell back, putting my books down and walking into the kitchen.

"I got two calls today. One from Janet's parents and another from the police. Janet's parents wanted to know if you've seen her. She went on a date a few nights ago and hasn't come home. I told them I would ask you when you got home. Have you seen Janet?"

"No mom, I haven't seen her. Sam and I went looking for her and Jeff. We did find his car out by the old Sanatorium…"

"Didn't my mom tell you to stay away from there?" she interrupts, angry.

"Yes, but Sam told Jeff that was a great place to go and make out," I reply as mom glares at me.

"Geez, when will kids learn? Do not go there again, understand?"

"Yes, mom."

"The police wanted me to tell you not to go there again either. There are no dead bodies in there. They checked."

"Yeah, they told us. I have to get to my homework," I reply, running upstairs and closing my room door.

"Two days later and still no word from Jeff or Janet?" I mumble to myself.

The next morning I head to the library to see what I can find out about the Sanitorium. Walking into the local history room, I seeing Sam already sitting. I grab a few books and page through them but can't find much on the Sanitarium.

"Hey, I found something. It says here they had a peak population of a hundred and seventy-five people. It opened in 1925 and closed in 1978. There's not much else."

"I'm looking at this one and it says the same thing. I wonder why there isn't anything more?" I ask.

"Amy, I think something bad happened there. I bet they're hiding whatever it is."

"I think so too. Let's ask Mrs. Charpoy. She may know something."

"We better hurry up then," he replies, looking at his watch.

We run to Sam's car and he drives like a lunatic, stopping in front of Bedford Road Collegiate. We run upstairs to the third floor and knock on the door.

"Well Hi, Amy. Sam. Are you here for detention?" Mrs. Charpoy asks, opening the door.

"No ma'am. We thought maybe you could help us. You see we're trying to find some information on the Sanatorium but we can't find much," I state as she welcomes us in.

"Come in and have a seat. I'll tell you what I know but remember not to plagiarize when you do the essay on this?"

"Uh, okay?" I answer, confused.

"Wait, we have to do an essay?" Sam asks.

"That's why you're looking for information, right?" she answers, looking at us confused.

"Ah, yes," I reply quickly to quell her suspicions.

"My father was a patient at the Sanatorium back in the sixties. There weren't many people there then, but there was a story of a doctor from the thirties that went around. This doctor liked experimenting on sick people. He was obsessed with finding a cure for tuberculosis and he would stop at nothing, including murder, to reach his goal. Dad did say that once they closed the doors to the Sanatorium in 1978 that Dr. Delve would be at rest again and no one would see him wandering the halls looking for new patients to experiment on. I was told the employees killed the doctor when they found out what he was doing, but this is a father's tale to his daughter. You can take it at what I said or make your own conclusions, the choice is yours."

"What happened to the doctor?" I ask, intrigued.

"I don't know. All my father would say was that he was glad to never see him again. They did seal that space up though. Built a wall. My guess would be to keep whatever he did quiet. I know they wanted to help people there, but who is going to help when something like that has happened?"

"Ok, thank you. That gives us something to work with," I answer, wondering why she looks upset.

"That's good. I'll give you a month to hand that in. That should be plenty of time to find out everything you can."

"Thanks, Mrs. Charpoy," I answer, turning and walking out of the room and down the hall.

"How the hell did asking a question get us an essay?" Sam asks, annoyed.

"I don't know Sam, but we should learn a lot," I reply, still hung up on the look on her face as she told us her father's story.

"Where are we going to find someone to help us, though?"

"Let's go see my grandma. She'll be able to tell us about what happened there."

Heading out of school, we get in Sam's car again. He looks at me and asks seriously, "She'll definitely know something?"

"She's told me, a lot about the old days," I answer as Sam peels away from the school.

We drive to my grandma's house and Sam hesitates once we get there. We walk up to the door and I ring the bell.

"Hello?" she answers the door with a smile.

"Hi Grandma, I hope you don't mind that I stopped by with my friend Sam," I answer.

"Oh, no dear. Come on in. What brings you here on a school day?" she asks, letting us in.

"Well, we have an assignment at school and our teacher Mrs. Charpoy said the only information we are going to find is from talking to people. I know you have told me some things, but maybe you can help us out."

"Yeah, I'm sure I can. Come on in to the living room."

"Wow. You sure have a lot of things Mrs. Cruz," Sam says, looking around.

"Yes, I have too much according to my husband."

I sit down on the couch with Sam beside me and Grandma sits in her rocking chair.

"So how can I help you?" she asks.

"You know that Sanatorium just over there?" I ask, pointing out the window.

"Yes?"

"We need to know everything about it?"

"I can't guarantee everything I know is correct. That was a long time ago."

"That's okay, anything would help us out." I respond, hopeful.

"Well, where would you like me to start?"

"I guess as far back as you can remember?"

"Well, when it first opened, there was an incredible need to put those TB patients somewhere away from everyone else. They were trying hard to stop the spread. All was good until the dirty thirties hit and there was suffering upon suffering. Some people were dying of TB while others were starving. There was a lack of quality doctors at the time so they were scraping the bottom of the barrel for lack of a better term. In 1931, my sister was taken there. She passed away in February of 1932. They would not let us see her after she was brought admitted. Any letters we were given said she was not being taken care of. By then, I was ten and I understood what was happening. We saw all the bodies coming out at night and knew something wasn't right."

"My dad fell sick in 1937. He spoke of a doctor who was there. He would come in and check on people, asking all sorts of personal questions. The people he took never came back. His last letter was saddening. He said this was his last letter and that he was fragile. The doctor said he was going to take him and try to cure him. He said he loved us all and he would see us on the other side. He was right, we never heard from him again. Anyways, that place did get better and so did the people. Less and less people were taken from their loved ones to this place. Finally, in 1978, the last person was released and they closed it down. We lived close enough that I swear we could hear screams coming from there. There were times I would swear on a bible there were lights on in that place. I know that place is haunted and I would say it is that doctor who took my father. I have seen kids playing in the building and I really want to say something, but I'm afraid something may happen to me if I do."

"I'm sorry grandma," I reply, watching her wipe her eyes.

"Not your fault. It was a different time than it is now."

"I'm sorry too. Did they ever catch that doctor doing those things to people?" Sam asks.

"Yes, but not by the police. The workers who cared for the people with TB caught him. If what I heard was right, they buried him in the basement where he did those awful things. The police questioned them before sealing the area up but nothing was ever said."

"So he's still in there?" I ask, worried.

"If what they said is true, yes. Don't you be going and checking out that place."

"I won't," I answer, trying to figure out what's true.

I get up to kiss her on the forehead before we walk back out to the car.

"Sam, do you think that's why the officer said they didn't check the basement?"

"Maybe. I think we should check that place out, but we should have more people there. Let's get a bunch of friends to also come."

"You better drop me off at home. I'll start making calls and tomorrow night we can get it started."

"Yeah. Tomorrow we will find out the truth, once and for all."

Driving to my house, we pass by the Sanatorium. "That place is creepier when the sun starts going down, isn't it?" I ask.

"Yeah, that defiantly has spook appeal."

Once we're outside my house, I pause for a moment. "Call me tomorrow and we'll see how many people will come with us."

"Yeah, I'll call you around noon."

#The Next day

I sit, waiting for Sam to call, as I wonder about what my grandma said. *"A mad doctor... could it be?"* The phone startles me as I jump up to get it, yelling "I got it!"

"Hello?" I say into the receiver.

"Hey, sorry I took a little longer than expected."

"No worries. Is everything still good?" I ask, watching my mom staring at me from the kitchen.

"I have five people willing to come with us. One says he knows about ghosts and stuff."

"That's great. Three? Yeah, I can be there around three," I answer, still watching as mom seems to become more curious by the second.

"What? Oh, your mom's right there. Got it. You have three people?"

"Yeah. Ok, I'll meet you around three at White's Pharmacy,"

"Yeah, no problem. I'll pick you up there at two."

"Awesome. Talk to you then," I hurriedly reply, hanging up the phone.

Mom looks at me with evil eyes, as I head back upstairs.

Two o'clock comes and I'm waiting at White's Pharmacy for Sam to arrive. Ten minutes later, he does.

"Sorry I'm late, I forgot the hammers. I brought a couple of sledgehammers too," he calls out the window.

"No problem. My friends are going to meet us there at seven tonight. They'll be waiting by the gate."

"Awesome. Mine will be there too. They said they'll bring some flashlights."

"Well, I guess we'll solve what the police can't," I state, grinning as Sam smiles back.

"I can't believe we are actually going to do this."

Getting in, we drive around for a while. "Where are we going, Sam?" I ask.

"I figured we'd stop at my uncle's place. He was in the sanatorium for a while."

"You think he'll have anything to say about it?" I ask as we drive down Confederation Drive and pull into a driveway.

"I know he will. He talks about how much that place changed him."

"Then why would you tell Jeff to take Janet there?" I ask, looking at Sam confused.

"I'll tell you, but don't tell anyone else. You see, I broke up with Ruby because of what Jeff and Janet told her about me. Honestly, I just wanted them to mind their own business."

"Yeah, but that seems like a harsh way to do that. Why wouldn't you just tell them to mind their own business?"

"Yeah, but you know me. My mouth opened and there it was."

"For your sake, I hope they're okay."

"Yeah, I guess that would be hard to live down if something did happen to them."

We get out, walk up to the door, and it opens as we get there.

"Hi, Uncle Rick," Sam greets the man.

Rick answers as he stares at me curiously,

"What brings you here, and who's your friend?"

"Hi, I'm Amy," I reply as he moves aside and we enter.

"Nice to meet you. Come on in and make yourselves at home."

"I was wondering if you would tell us about your experience at the Sanatorium?" Sam asks.

Rick grimaces as he looks at us both. "I guess I could. Why do you want to know?"

"School. We are doing an essay on the Sanatorium, but we can't seem to find much about it."

"If it's going to help your education, I will."

"Thank you, mister Elroy." I reply.

"You're welcome, Amy. I spent two months in that hellhole. I went there back in sixty-three when I was fourteen. The people who took me there said they helped a lot of people get better. They neglected to mention what a person would have to endure there. When I first arrived, they poked and prodded me as if I were an animal. I know they had to do it, but there was no compassion. I might as well have been in jail. They got us out of our street clothes and assigned our spaces. Mine was in the hallway on the second floor. So many people were dead and just left there. Nobody removed them. There were a few there that would come by often, but they were not always working. Those days, we got everything we needed to make us feel comfortable. Other days we only got basic help. I honestly believe they would have rather we died. I was in the hallway for days and they just kept passing me by."

"There was no privacy at all. I remember talking to a woman who was in front of me. She was so upset about being left out there. She was finally moved somewhere else and a few days later I was transferred to a room. The nurse I had made me feel like everything was going to be ok. The nurse on the shift after that made me feel like I was nothing more than a burden."

"After being in there for a month, I honestly could not wait to die. I had no choice but to look at the dead people around you every day. A nurse would come in and take blood, or see if you were still breathing. The smell was one of the worst things there. You could not avoid the putrid smell of death. When I did get out, I swore to myself, I would never step foot in another hospital as long as I lived. You cannot forget what happened there. You could drink beer twenty-four hours a day and not forget. That is how bad it was there. I still have nightmares about that place."

"Wow, that's bad. Did anything else happen there?" Sam asks.

"Yeah, but I don't think that's age appropriate," Rick says, rubbing his beard.

"You can tell us, Mr. Elroy. I am sure we have heard worse," I reply watching his eye twitching.

"I don't know about that, but if you want to hear it all I'll tell you more."

"We want as much information as we can get," Sam says.

"Well, a few doctors would tell us how we were going to die anyway. These people only really concerned themselves with not getting too close. There were many times where they would not check on us. I don't know if they didn't have the staff or if they just didn't care. I think a lot of them treated us like lab rats. They would poke and prod us at any given time, morning, noon or night. That place was the definition of hell. I am sorry, but that is all I am going to say. I'm going to have nightmares for weeks to come."

"That's ok, you gave us lots to go on," I respond.

"Yeah, I think I want to be alone, please."

"No problem. Thank you again," I answer, nudging Sam to move towards the door.

Walking out the door, we hear Sam's uncle break down in tears. By the time we reach the car, we hear something crash. "Is your uncle going to be ok?" I ask, concerned.

"I think so. We better get out of here."

We get in the car, Sam backs out of the driveway, and we head to meet our friends at the Sanatorium.

Forgotten Past

We get there around 6:30, but no one is there yet. The gate is still open but we wait for the others. People start showing, and closer to seven there are six of us. Nobody knows where the other two are, but we carry everything to the back of the sanatorium. There is a locked chain on the door now.

"Damn. Good thing I brought the bolt cutters," Sam smiles, pulling them from his gym bag.

Snapping the chain in two, he takes it off, and we carry everything inside.

"Look, there's a path over there. What do you think that was for?" Ryan asks.

"I don't know. I didn't see it there before," Sam answers.

We bring our attention back to the task and try to get organized.

"Ok, so how do we want to do this? Are we all staying together?" Sam asks.

"I think we should all stay together, Sam." I reply, turning my flashlight on.

"Ok, then it's settled, we'll stay together. Let's make our way downstairs. The cops said they couldn't get down there. Let's see why."

I make my way to the end of the hall. We sound like a heard of elephants in the quiet building. Sam looks around before opening the door, and we walk around to find a wide-open set of stairs.

"What the hell? The stairs aren't blocked. Those cops were lying. I bet they didn't want to check it out. Let's go."

Everyone else turns on their flashlights, and we go down the stairs to the basement. The eerie sound of water dripping echoes down the hall.

"I wonder what they did down here?" Kara whispers.

"I don't know Kara, but whatever they did stunk," Tim replies.

Kara shines her light around and stops, "Look, there's a wall over there."

Sam also shines his light across the wall, "it looks newer than the building. I wonder if it is true what the employees did to that doctor. It sounds like there was a doctor who went crazy and was killing people until the employees killed him."

"Bull shit," Ryan shouts.

"No, I'm serious. That's what we were told. Right, Amy?"

"Yeah. I didn't think much about it until now, though."

"You mean there's some freak behind this wall?" James responds, frightened.

"Yes, James. He is going to come for you," Sam laughs.

Everyone bursts out laughing, and I walk towards the wall. I feel around but it seems solid.

"Stand back, I'm going to smack this wall," Sam says, pulling out a sledgehammer.

I watch him from a distance as he swings hard and a couple of bricks shift slightly. A few more swings and four blocks fall out of place, letting a stagnate smell escape.

"That stinks!" Sam stops, covering his nose.

After another a few more round of hits, it finally opens up enough for a person to pass through. We shine the flashlights into the darkness revealing the horror.

"Oh my god. Look at that over there," James gasps.

"What is that? A lab of some sort?" Sam adds.

We walk through the open wall, shining the lights in front of us. The sight is gruesome. There are bones and clothes spread out in a neat pile.

"Those clothes look old," Ryan states.

"So do all these tools. They look almost medieval," Sam says.

"It smells rotten down here," Kara gags.

"Look, there's a hole in this wall!" Sam says, shining his light towards it.

"Jesus!" I shout, looking inside.

"What is it, Amy?"

"There are bones in here. I don't know if they're human or not, but there are a lot of small bones."

"Wow, you think your grandma was right, Amy?" Sam asks.

"God, I hope not Sam."

"What are you two talking about?" Serena interrupts.

"My grandma said there was a doctor here who liked to experiment on people. She said they avenged these people by killing the doctor down here and sealing up the wall." I explain.

"So, what you are saying is you two lead us on a wild goose chase to validate what your grandmother said?" James interrupts.

"Yes and no. We are trying to find out what happened to Jeff and Janet, but everyone we talk with has something different to say about this place."

"I'm leaving, who's with me?" James says.

"I'm staying. It's not every day you get to see something like this," Serena shrugs.

"Me too," Sam adds. "Go if you want, James, but the five of us are staying here."

We watch James walk back through the wall, and the light from his flashlight dims as he disappears down the hallway. We start looking around again but are interrupted by a scream from upstairs.

"That idiot is trying to scare us," Sam says.

We stop and listen as the screams continue before Sam gets flustered and throws the sledgehammer down.

"You know what? Enough of James doing this. Let's go kick this guy's ass."

"Yeah! Let's do it," Kara shouts.

We make our way back to the hole in the wall, and use our flashlights to quickly walk up the stairs. We hear another scream, and this time it sounds like someone saying 'no'.

"It's coming from upstairs," I state.

We run up to the second floor, and the light dims as the sun creeps down in the west. Sam leads us down the hall, until we stop at the room at the end of the corridor. Sam holds his hand up.

"Don't look," he answers. "James wasn't trying to scare us."

"What is it, Sam?" I ask, feeling like I already know.

"It looks like someone wanted to see what was inside of him."

"Who's in here with us?" Kara asks, looking around frightened.

"Show yourself!" Sam shouts.

"Get out before it's dark! The doctor is coming for you!" a woman's voice whispers from the encroaching darkness.

We whip around to see where the voice is coming from and see an image of a nurse dressed in a uniform from the 1930s or 40s.

"Who are you?" I ask, scared.

"The doctor is coming for you. He is mad. Get out while you still can," she responds.

"What doctor?" Serene asks, shaking.

"Doctor Delve. He went mad looking for a cure. Get out now or you'll be forsaken here."

We look at each other, confused, as she keeps telling us to leave. Going into the room, we grab James but an ominous growl makes us drop him. In the corner of the hall, two red eyes peer out of the darkness, sending us all running out of the room. We run straight through the nurse and down the stairs to the door at the far end of the main floor. Once outside, we look back at the building before running for our cars. I try to put as much distance between us and the Sanatorium as I can.

"Ok. We all have to promise not to say anything about what happened here," Sam pants between gasps for air. "We'll all go to jail for murder. Nobody is going to believe a ghost killed James."

"I promise. I'm never coming back here again," Kara whimpers.

"Let's just get out of here," Ryan says, looking back at the Sanatorium.

I hop in with Sam and we all drive off.

"Holy shit, Sam. I don't think Jeff and Janet are alive." I say, watching as the Sanatorium disappears in the distance.

"You think? Did you see James? His head was split open. I think those eyes were the devil."

"Let's never speak of that place again," I yell back.

"Shit!" Sam yells, slamming the steering wheel with his hand. "I left everything in the basement."

"Leave it."

"My dad is going to be so mad. I lost all his hammers."

"Do you really, want to go back there?" I ask, hesitantly.

"Screw it. I'll buy my dad, new ones."

The doctor is in

Dr. Stephen Delve;

June 12th, 1931

I started as a physician at the Sanatorium today. Everything ran smoothly. A few people trickled in here and there.

August, 1931

Forgotten Past

There is a steady stream of people coming in. We're treating the symptoms, but we're not looking for a cure. With the drought and TB combined, people are getting sick without proper nutrition. Some people were misdiagnosed and forced to stay the term.

November

We have a no visitor policy in place. We still have trespassers who wander onto the grounds and they're obliged to remain afterwards. Sometimes I feel they did it to get a free meal. There are so many people, and at times the work is never ending.

December

This is hell itself. Between the cold, the sick, and the food shortages, we're choosing on a case-by-case basis. The healthier ones are given more, and the others are given less.

April, 1932

We're nothing more than empty shells of our former selves. There are so many dead and nothing we can do to help them. I made a promise to myself that I will find a cure. My every waking hour is spent helping people and trying to find something to cure this bringer of death.

May, 1932

I took my first person to the basement. I felt horrible and exhausted, but I had to find a cure. So many people are dying. I cut him open and found he not only had infected lungs but also had other infections spread through his body. I cut open his skull, knowing the brain contained the most valuable information. After exploring twenty people, I have composed a theory. TB seems to die with the patients. If I can figure a way to get this to occur in a living person, then they should get better quicker. Maybe injecting medication inside the eye socket would allow the fluid to get to the brain and fight it better.

June, 1932

I have broken a couple of walls to hide the people I am experimenting on. I'm being questioned about why so many people have gone missing. There are 62 people down here and I can't move them to the morgue or they'd be noticed. The space I have is between the walkways where anyone can go. I cannot afford to move them anywhere but these walls. I feel I am getting closer to finding a cure. The more people experiment with, the more I learn how this bacterium works. When I locate the treatment, the deaths will be worth it.

September, 1932

I have only slept two hours a night since I began here. I feel I understand more of my mistakes and am rectifying the problems.

Opening their heads, and letting them bleed out is the missing piece of the puzzle I was not able to figure out. I can't believe I didn't see it before. I have spent so much time and it was right in front of me all along.

October, 1932

Unbelievable, I cannot believe they want me to stop. They say I am crazy, but they just want the credit for my work. I can see it now, they get the praise and I get nothing! Well, I see I must be brave. I must stand alone in the face of my enemy. I fear they are going to steal my work. I must get it done quickly to ensure I get the credit. I will arrange to have ten people brought down here tonight. These ten will provide the results of my testing. I can hand my work in and get the credit I deserve.

October 28th

How dare those doctors and nurses! All my work is gone. They stole it. Those greedy bastards threatened me. I am not crazy, I am a genius. No one else figured out that by draining all the blood, the person can be cured. I am going to get them. I will get them all for this.

November 1st

I fear this entry will be my last entry. As of this morning, my fellow colleagues tried to put a restraining jacket on me. They have chased me... Oh my, they are here now...

Present Day

I grab James off the floor, and he twitches from the extraction of blood. I carry him to the stairs as the elevator hasn't worked in years and he moans with every step. "Don't worry James, soon you'll be cured."

In the basement, I lay him down on a gurney.

"It hurts," he whispers.

"Don't worry," I reply, strapping him down. "You'll be cured soon."

The blood continues to seep from his forehead. I pick up a rusty scalpel and bone saw just as James starts convulsing. Placing my instruments on his chest, I check for a pulse.

"I lost another one. There must be a way to save these people... so many deaths... WHY?" I shout, throwing my instruments against the wall.

I unstrap James and carry him to the wall, throwing him inside. Turning sharply, I hear voices.

"Eli, we shouldn't be in here."

"Don't worry, Kalvin. Who's going to know?"

"*Another chance to redeem myself*," I think, as I listen to the voices come closer. I walk towards the stairs and tap on the wall, listening.

"Did you hear that Eli?"

I tap louder.

"Yeah, was that coming from downstairs?"

I tap a couple more times.

"Let's check it out."

Their footsteps creep down the dark staircase.

"I can't see anything," Eli whispers.

I see the first boy is around ten and he's standing within grasp. The other boy comes into my view and he is around the same age.

"I can't see anything. It's too dark. Let's go back upstairs."

I reach out and grab them both by their necks. "Don't worry, I'll help you two. Soon you'll be cured."

I carry them to my gurneys and start to strap them down.

"Who the hell are you?" one of them screams.

"Don't worry, I'm here to help you. I'm Dr. Delve," I reply, as he tries to crawl away from me. The other stays still, paralyzed with fear. "Don't worry... I'll fix you."

"Help!" he screams. "I can't see you, Eli."

I grab my scalpel with one hand and Eli's forehead with the other, and make an incision from temple to temple. He screams.

"Don't worry, soon you'll be better," I whisper, patting his arm. I turn to Kalvin. I walk up to him, and grab his arm but he punches and kicks at me.

"Please, I'm not sick. Let me go!"

"Kalvin, you're sick. Everyone who comes here is sick. Don't worry, you'll be good as new when I'm finished," I reply, patting his chest.

I turn to his friend who is convulsing and walk over to him, whispering. "Hang on, you'll be cured soon." He gasps for air so I go grab the bone saw. I rip his shirt off as he continues to convulse and cut his ribs open in an attempt to help him breathe.

"Come on, damn it! Breathe!" Kalvin shouts,

"Your friend is in distress, he'll be fine," I reply as Kalvin continues to shout.

"You sick bastard... you killed him!"

"No, I'm curing him," I say as Eli stops moving.

"Eli...?"

"He can't answer. I failed to save him," I answer.

Amy's school.

I glance up to see Amy standing in front of me, looking worried.

"Mrs. Charpoy?" she speaks up.

"Yes, Amy?" I reply, watching her tear up.

"I have something I have to get off my chest. We went to the Sanatorium a couple of days ago. We found a wall in the basement and when we tore through it, and the smell was awful..."

"Why did you go there? I said you wouldn't find much information about it. I didn't say go to the Sanatorium and check it out?" I respond, worried.

"We were looking for a couple of friends who went missing there…"

"You mean Jeff and Janet?"

"Yes…"

"As much as you want to find people, sometimes not opening things is better. I told you about that place because I thought you wanted information to use for your essay. Sit down and tell me exactly what happened. What do you mean you tore through the wall?"

"We took hammers and broke through the wall in the basement."

"I see. You should not have done that, Amy…"

"I know, but something with red eyes took James. We got out of there quick and vowed not to go back."

"Good. Don't worry about it. Just don't go there again," I answer, knowing what I'm going to have to do.

"I promise we won't."

"Go back to your class," I answer.

3:30 arrives and I look at the phone. I pick up the receiver and dial, listening to it ring.

"Hello?" Anna answers.

"Hey sis, what's up?" I ask, trying to figure a way to tell her about what happened.

"Not a lot. I was just getting ready to go out this evening."

"We have one thing to do before that."

"Karen, don't you say it. Don't say it."

"A couple students of mine. They broke the wall down," I whisper.

"Are you kidding me?" she yells.

"I wish I were."

"I don't want to deal with this. You go alone this time."

"I need you there, too."

"Fine, I'll meet you there in an hour," she growls.

I hang up the phone and quickly pack my papers to leave. I close the classroom door behind me and walk out of the school. I head home to grab a quick bite and wash up. Looking in the mirror, I shake my head in disbelief that it has happened again. Finally, I leave my apartment and go back to my car.

"I hope Anna is there. I can't do this alone," I think to myself.

Driving towards the sanatorium, memories of yesterday keep popping in and out of my head. Finally, I pull up behind Anna's car. She's standing there, leaning against her car, looking at me with a look that says I'm in trouble. I get out and walk over to her, giving her a hug. "Are you ready?" I whisper.

"No, but let's go."

We walk to the building, and I feel as if someone is watching me. Climbing the ramp at the back of the building, we stop at the door. I look to Anna and take a deep breath as I open the door and head inside. Just as the door closes, a scream echoes down the hall. Running to the end of the hall, we go through the door and down the stairs. I turn my flashlight on.

"He must have another person down there with him. Let's go," Anna yells.

Running through the wall, we see two boys on gurneys. One is dead and the other screaming.

"Grandpa! Please stop!" I scream. He stops and looks confused, turning towards me. A grin comes across his face.

"Karen. Anna. I'm helping these boys get better."

I hold my hands out towards him, stepping closer to the gurney with the screaming boy. "Grandpa, you're done helping these people. Tuberculous isn't running rampant anymore. They have medicines to deal with it. Please, let this boy go. You should be resting now."

His eyes glow red as he stands on the opposite side of the gurney, looking at the rusty scalpel in his bloody hand.

"I can't rest now. Too many sick people need help. This boy needs me to fix him."

"Grandpa, please let this boy go. He isn't sick. If you try to fix him, you're going to kill him. Please?" I whisper, untying a leg strap.

"I can't. There are so many sick people coming here. They never stop coming."

"Please let the boy go. We'll stay and help you," I reply, untying an arm strap. Slowly he lowers the scalpel and it makes a clinking sound on the metal table. He unstraps the boy.

"Get out, now."

The boy looks fearful, but jumps up and runs away as fast as he can. Anna shines the flashlight towards him, and he disappears through the wall. Our grandfather stands there, looking defeated.

"I don't understand. Why am I here if they have medicine?" he whispers.

"You spent your whole life trying to stop tuberculous from killing innocent people. Grandma told us about how after your sister Karen died of tuberculous you swore to eradicate this disease from the history books. Grandma believed you'd continue long after you died to try to defeat this," I answer, holding my hand towards him.

"Karen was so young when it took her. I remember my son saying he would name his daughter after my sister. I can see her eyes in you, Karen." He places his hand in mine.

"Grandpa, you're dead. You should be resting now," I say as Anna grabs his other hand.

"It's okay to rest," Anna adds. "You have done the best you can. Your work at the Sanatorium is finished. Rest and know you've done all you can do here."

He Looks over at Anna and squeezes our hands softly.

"I don't feel dead. I feel alive…"

"You died a long time ago. Remember? The last time we came here, in 1979, we had this same talk," I reply.

"That was a long time ago."

"We came to put you to rest. What brought you back this time?" I ask.

"There were a couple of sick teenagers. I tried to help them."

"No. You murdered those children. All of them were students at the school where I teach."

"Why did they come here if they weren't sick? I don't understand."

"Now that the Sanatorium is closed, you are going to get people coming around here who aren't sick," I try to explain.

"But there are so many people still here. They can't close it until all the people here are cured."

"You were a good doctor when you were alive. Mom told us what happened to you. She said you were really trying to help the people who came here. She said after a few months you changed and were determined to find a cure. You started experimenting with individuals who were sick. She told me you went mad and the employees killed you and buried you here. You were a good doctor, but this place got to you."

"Yes, I remember now," he lowers his head. "So many people died. I could not keep up with the demand for help. Yes, I thought I could cure them."

"We know what it must have been like for you. There was so much pressure to regain control of the outbreak. Nobody blames you for what happened in the past, but you are killing innocent people now."

"I was just trying to help," he weeps.

"We know, but you need to rest. Your work is done here," Anna says softly.

"There are so many people still here…"

"Don't worry, they died here. Perhaps they cannot move on. You are all stuck here. We have tried to get you all moved on, but this place binds you here. You have to learn that people are going to come here to check out the building, or to just come around. You need to leave these people alone," I continue, sternly.

"I try, but the urge to help far outweighs my need to rest."

"Yes, but you must sleep. Your work on earth is finished," Anna adds.

"Tell us where they buried you and we can move you to a new place," I reply.

"I can't. No one will ever find me."

"You can tell us, grandpa. You can trust us." I respond, watching his tears fall onto the gurney.

"In the floor under the wall. Where they broke through," he whispers, pointing to the bottom of the wall near the corner.

"We'll get you out of here grandpa. I promise," Anna smiles.

We grabbing a couple of hammers and hit the wall, slowly breaking pieces off. Three hours later, Anna breaks through the floor. I help her dig the dirt from the hole in the floor until we find the remains of our grandfather. His skeleton is still wearing a white lab coat. We pick up each bone and place them in a bag. We turn to grandpa when we're finished.

"Thank you," he whispers.

Pankratz

Grandpa disappears as Anna picks up the last bone. We head up the stairs and a calming feeling comes over the entire building. We place the bones in the trunk of my car and drive to the funeral home to give him the sendoff he deserved.

Peace resided for a while, but the spirits became restless again, and by late 1989 the city of Saskatoon tore down the Sanatorium building, claiming it was beyond repair.

This story is based on bits of knowledge from a man who was at the Sanatorium for a short part of his life. His stay was a nightmare for him. This story depicts all sides: the patients, doctors, nurses, and family members. I will not claim everything contained within these pages is truth of the goings on while the Sanatorium was open, but rather my own thoughts while putting on each of their shoes, and spending some time living a day in theirs. Some people may view my thoughts as biased, but I have included the patients, nurses, and doctors, along with friends and family viewpoints. This story is informed by the experience of A.P., the man who actually was at the Sanatorium when it was open, and my own experiences after it closed in 1978 until it was torn down in 1989.

The patient's POV is that of a nightmarish living horror. I am sure they went in with the hope of being cured. Once there for days, or weeks, the reality of what they would have to endure set in. In the early days of the Sanatorium, people died on a daily basis. This would be their lives until either they got better, or passed on. The patients, who may have screamed in pain, caused mental stress on others. One day you may meet someone who is scared to step foot in a hospital. If they were born before 1978, this might be the reason. This is the story of the man I know, and will never forget.

The doctor's POV is from the patient, family, and from co-workers. Truthfully, it was not meant to be anything more than what people saw. You get into healthcare because you want to help others. I am sure these nurses and doctors intended to do just that. Let's face it though, watching people suffering and dying takes a toll on both your mental and physical health, creating the pullback effect. The doctors and nurses would have been swamped, and at some point, I am sure the doctors and nurses lost it. I have tried to put myself in their spot, but it always plays out the same. Eventually, no matter how many you save, the ones you lose always on your mind. I do have great respect for these individuals as it takes a lot of courage to face an unknown death. They stepped in when nobody else would.

The families had little to no communication with the patients. A photo of them, when they were feeling good, but no pictures when they were not doing well. I know it would pain me to no ends if one of my children had to go through that. We take for granted everything we have now. Before cell phones and the internet, when this was happening, they had cameras, pens, paper, and landlines. I am sure that these were readily available, but if the patient was not doing well,

I doubt anyone had the time to help. The worry that must have gone on was probably stressful, not knowing if your loved one was going to come home again.

The absolute truth is unknown to me. I wish I could say without a doubt what happened there, but I cannot. A bedside telling is all I have. I have met a few people who are deathly afraid to step one foot into a hospital. Can I say they all have the same story? I could, but that would not be the truth. My biggest regret is not asking everyone. Before 2001, I didn't really care to know why. Now, it is too late for me to ask these people as they have expired and taken their answers with them. Most people are willing to talk, but only if you are ready to listen to their words. I would like to tell the city they're wrong for tearing the Sanatorium down. The city is afraid of the unknown, and would rather tear it down than let it become part of our history.

Perry Pankratz February 5th, 2017

Just another day

July 1983 was when Jeff, Darren, and myself, Perry Pankratz, had our first encounter with the Saskatoon Sanatorium. That's a day I have yet to forget. We were riding our bikes along the grooved tire tracks on the west side of the tree line. As we got closer to the path, the building itself was enough to give you the creeps. An uneasy feeling came over me when I saw the back windows of the building. Most of the windows were broken, and I could swear every window had someone looking out of them. At eleven, and twelve years old, we did not realize at the time what they were. Some looked like they had bandages, others looked mutilated. We thought the place was still open. The people looked so real.

We continued to ride down the path and came out on the east side of the Sanatorium. This trail was a wicked one. The path itself was three feet wide and rough. The trail swerved from the left to right, with a hill and then a big dip. As you got to the top, it split into two paths. One went along the fence line of the golf course behind the sanatorium. The other made a sharp left and then turned east again. When both paths met again, it was on an uphill.

The ground was mainly sandy here. If you managed to get to the top of that hill still on your bike, you were doing good. Ninety percent of the time your bicycle tire bit into the sand and you were thrown to the ground. After that hill, it was dirt again and you came out on the east side of the Sanatorium. We went once, just as a test run. Our game was to go through. The rule was if your feet touched the ground, or you had to push your bike, you had to keep going through until you made it.

Being young, dumb, and stupid at the time, we spent most of the day going down that path. Each time it was something different.

On my second attempt, I hit a root and face planted into the path. Jeff was behind and stopped to help me up. I had a bloody nose.

Once we got to the top of the hill, we started again. Darren, in the lead took the path on the right while Jeff and I took the left path. We heard, Darren yell while we were riding, and when we met up, he said it felt like he had been punched in the chest. He lifted his shirt, and his chest was red.

We continued this for most of the day, but each time was something different happened. There was getting pushed off your bike, the front tire turning and wiping out, or not being able to turn. Between everything that had happened, we walked our bikes home because they were as banged up as we were.

A few days later, we tried to finish what we started, but had the same results. After being beaten by that path so many times, we decided to just explore. We found a little offshoot of a path. It wasn't very big, maybe a foot wide, and was mainly covered with overgrowth. We followed the route that headed towards the west side fence and it took us to a little opening. There was a half-buried outhouse there. We continued to play in those woods, all summer.

That was the last time I had been there. I cannot speak for Jeff or Darren. I moved that fall to the East side of Saskatoon. I have not spent a lot of time thinking about it, but there are times where I cannot stop thinking about that place, knowing what I know now.

A.P.

In 2001, I had the pleasure of talking to a man who was a patient at the Saskatoon Sanatorium, knowing he was dying from cancer of the veins. He did not mention the date he was there, but said his older brother died there. He told me some of what happened to him, but I do not think he told me everything. He made mention of hating hospitals. He confided in me that the reason he hated hospitals so much was because of what happened to him in the Sanatorium.

Some doctors and nurses cared, and some did not. He never mentioned names to me. He said it depended on the day or shift. The decent ones were always trying to keep their spirits up, while the others said they were going to die. They did surgery on him, and put a piece of his shoulder blade in his neck.

The nurses at St. Paul's hospital kept trying to keep the door closed, almost as if they wanted to quarantine him. He was in a room of his own and seemed happier when the door was open. He talked about being a lab rat, but the look on his face told me it was something he did not want to remember. I left shortly after that.

Going back a few days later, he was not the same man. He was cheery and trying to be happy. He mentioned how he was nearing the end without saying it outright. He did say that he wished he could have been home instead of the hospital. He brought up that there was a doctor at the Sanatorium who seemed different then the other doctors. I took that to mean he was a mad doctor.

We talked for hours until it was time to go. Sadly, that was the last time I got to speak with him. He passed away a day or two later. Rest in peace, A.P.

Forgotten Past

July 16, 1945

Walking through the cemetery gates, she passes by a sign that reads "Woodlawn Cemetery", and makes her way to a newly dug grave. The sun gives way to the few clouds that pass by. She kneels down by a headstone that reads "Raymond Church". Annabelle brushes away some of the leaves from last night's storm as tears trickle down her cheeks. She places a single rose on top of his headstone.

"I miss you so much, uncle. Not a day goes by where I don't think about you."

She runs her finger along his name and a blast of cold wind blows across the headstone. She grabs the rose and holds it in her hand. As the wind settles down again, she places it back on the headstone. Standing up from the icy chill of the wind, she looks around.

"Annabelle, come quick," a sinister voice whispers.

Turning towards the voice, Annabelle sees a dark, shadowy mist standing in front of the trees. Her heart pound as it motions for her to come to him. Annabelle shakes her head but he continues motioning for Annabelle to come to him again more insentiently. Looking away from him, she sees a group of shadowing men coming towards her. Her heart races, and slowly she makes her way towards the shadowy figure.

"Annabelle, these men are coming to hurt you. Walk through these trees and you'll be safe, I promise," the voice whispers once she's closer.

The men begin running toward her, and one shouts, "I have something to ask you!"

"Run through the trees and save yourself from this inevitable death. Run now or die in this cemetery!" the voice urges.

Annabelle shakes uncontrollably as she sees the men closing in. She looks into the eyes of the dark mist motioning for her to go through the trees.

She makes her way through the trees and vanishes.

July 16, 2000.

Forgotten Past

Emerging from the trees, Annabelle seems dazed and confused as she falls to the ground. Grabbing her head like she has a headache, she lets out a pained groan. After a few minutes of rolling around, she slowly gets to her feet, shaking off the headache. She looks around for the men but is even more confused. Everything seems different. People are dressed funny and there are more graves. Even the air smells different. Looking back at her Uncle's grave, she notices it's more weathered.

"What's going on? This looks like Woodlawn, but yet it doesn't."

Making her way to the entrance, people look at her as if she belongs in a circus. Some of them point and laugh as she passes by. When she reaches the road, a police car pulls up beside her.

"Excuse me, Miss? Are you all right? You look lost?" a heavyset man in a police uniform calls out.

Annabelle looks at the police car, and her eyes widen in fright.

"What's your name, miss?"

Annabelle looks at him fearfully as he leans over to the passenger side of the car. She

"Annabelle Church."

The officer punches something into his computer as he eyeballs Annabelle. "All right, can you tell me where you live?"

"1514 First Avenue North," Annabelle replies, distracted by the world around her. The shapes and colours are new.

The officer opens the passenger side door, and Annabelle jumps back, frightened.

"Are you on something miss? You seem quite jumpy. Hop in and I'll give you a ride home."

Annabelle's face went pale. Her mom and dad always said you can trust a police officer. This police officer didn't look like a police officer though. Police cars don't have red and blue lights.

"My parents said never to accept rides from strangers. I'll just walk home. Thank you anyways."

Before the officer could say anything, Annabelle quickly turned towards First Avenue, but he pulled up beside her again.

"It's against the law to walk away from an officer that's questioning you."

Coming to a stop, Annabelle looks at the angry police officer. Unsure of what to do, she pleads, "I just want to go home. I haven't done anything wrong."

"I'm sorry if I came off harsh. My name is Vincent Reece. Please just get in the car and I'll drive you home. Okay?"

"Please, I just live up there. I'll just walk home."

"Alright, but I am going to follow you home and talk to your parents, okay?"

Annabelle nods and continues her way up First Avenue. The police car drives ahead and parks in front of her house. The officer is standing on the sidewalk by the time Annabelle arrives. As Annabelle turns to look at her house, she stops and gasps.

"What's wrong, Annabelle," he asks, walking over.

"What happened to my house? What's going on?" she whispers.

The police officer looks at the house, then at Annabelle's face. "What do mean? The house looks perfectly fine to me."

Annabelle slowly turns her head towards the officer as she looks to find the words to explain. The door opens and an older woman comes out.

"Excuse me officer, is there something I can help you with?"

"Yes, are you Annabelle's mother?"

Before the lady can respond, Annabelle stares at her angrily. "She's not my mother. Where's my mom and what are you doing in my house?"

The look on the lady's face turns sour as she replies, "What do you mean your house? I've lived here since 1997, and I've never seen you around here before."

The officer looks bewildered, as he looks between Annabelle and the woman standing at the door. He steps in between them.

"What is your name ma'am?"

"Jasmine Smith. I can prove I've lived here since 1997, just give me a moment and I'll be back"

Jasmine comes out a few minutes later and the officer grabs the paper from Jasmine hands him.

"Thank you, everything seems to be in order. Annabelle, I'm sorry but Jasmine has lived here since 1997. Are you sure this is your house?"

"Yes, I'm sure this is my house. I've lived here since I was born in 1929."

The officer looks at Annabelle strangely.

"I don't know what you're smoking lady, but I suggest you get help," Jasmine shouts.

"I'm sorry, ma'am, please go back in your house. I'll take care of the Annabelle here," the officer states, handcuffing Annabelle.

As walks back into her house, the officer holds Annabelle's arm as he escorts her to the police car.

"Why am I in handcuffs? Jasmine's the one who should be in handcuffs. She's in my parents' house right now. Why?"

As he starts driving, he looks in the rearview mirror at Annabelle who is glaring at him.

"I'm sorry, Annabelle. Jasmine had all the rental information for that house. Can you tell me exactly what was different about your house, other than Jasmine living there?"

"The paint job was different. Everything was different. Ever since that shadow mist man nothing has been right. People are dressed different, cars are different, and everything's different. You say it's 2000 but I know it's 1945! What's going on? Are you all playing a sick joke on me? Is this Billy's doing?"

The officer looks at Annabelle through the rearview mirror, watching the tears trickling down her face. He sighs as he tries to figure out what's going on with her.

"What about this Billy? What do you think he's done?"

"He's a boy I refused to go out with a few weeks ago. He told me he'd get back at me. I just don't know how he pulled off changing everything."

The officer looks worried about Annabelle's mental state. He drove to the psychiatric hospital and pulled up to the front doors.

"Annabelle? I'm really worried about you. I think something traumatic happened. I brought you to a psychiatric hospital. These people are going to take care of you, and help you figure out what's going on."

"I'm not crazy! I know exactly what day it is, and everything else. You can't do this to me."

The officer shakes his head, getting out of the car. Walking around to the other side, he opens the door and grabs Annabelle's arm. He fights to get her out of the back seat, but eventually gets her in a wheelchair. They walk through the doors and to the front desk.

"Who do we have here, officer?" the nurse asks.

Forgotten Past

"Her name is Annabelle Church and she believes its 1945. I think something traumatic may have happened to her. If you could check her out and make sure she's alright, I'll be grateful."

"No problem, officer. We'll get her taken care of. Just sign here and we're good to go."

He signed the release papers, as and two orderlies wheel Annabelle down a hallway. Along the way, Annabelle overhears the nurse say something about schizophrenia, and possible delusions. Struggling to remove the restraints with no success, Annabelle's fear grows as they wheel her into a room.

As the orderlies and nurse talk amongst themselves, Annabelle knows she has only one chance to get out of here. Waiting until they unbuckle the restraints on her arms, Annabelle quickly reaches and scratches one of their faces.

As the other orderly tries to grab her hands, Annabelle bites deep into his arm. Unaware the nurse is loading a hypodermic needle, Annabelle continues to fight these two orderlies. There's only a quick poke in her arm before she goes limp.

Waking up hours later, Annabelle tries to move finds herself tied to the bed. As she looks at the ceiling tiles, she begins to wonder if her father was right about what he said about people. Soon after, a man in a white coat comes and sits down beside the bed. His grey hair reminds her of dirty snow.

"I'm Dr. Steen, and I'm going to ask you a few questions. Just answer them honestly. Is your name Annabelle Church?"

Annabelle nods. "Yes, but I don't belong here. When can I leave?"

The doctor smiles as he writes something down.

"Well, first we have to find out what the problem is. It says here you seem to think it's 1945? Can you explain why you believe it's 1945?"

"I don't know what you're playing at. As I said to police officer, I was visiting my Uncle's grave whom we buried last month. I had walked through a couple of trees, and next thing I know everything has changed. The cars are different, people are dressed funny, and now I'm tied down to this damn bed!" Annabelle glares at the doctor.

"So you're saying you were at the cemetery and when you walked through a couple of trees, you were in a different time? Interesting indeed. Well Annabelle, I can assure you it is July 16, 2000. If you look at your clothing, you are the one who is out of place. I would like to run some tests to confirm what you're saying."

"No! I don't want any tests done. I just want to find a way home. I don't want to be here anymore. Please just let me go."

The doctor scribbles in his notepad, occasionally glancing up at Annabelle. As he looks at the paperwork he has, he looks thoughtful.

"Annabelle? Do you know why you were brought here? We believe you're mentally ill. You're telling a tale that's just unbelievable. After we conduct a few tests, we should be able to release you within a few days."

Annabelle glares at the doctor with a new-found hatred. She turns away and looks at the wall as she answers. "I want to get out of here now. You have no right to hold me here."

"I don't think you understand Annabelle. You don't have a choice in this matter. You were brought here by a police officer, and that means you were brought here to be assessed for mental capacity. After we have concluded that you are, or are not insane, you will be released."

"I'm not insane. I know what day it is, and I know what year it is."

Hearing the shouting, a nurse enters the room and pokes Annabelle in the arm with another needle.

"I'm sorry, Annabelle, but we aren't playing games here. We are in the year 2000. 1945 was 55 years ago, and there's no way someone as young as you is 55. Now, get some rest and we will talk more in a few hours."

Annabelle's eyes have a hard time focusing on the doctor as her words slur and everything fades to a whisper.

Dr. Steen's office

The doctor quickly closes his door as he hurriedly makes his way to the desk. Going through his rolodex, he finds the man he's looking for. Suspiciously keeping an eye on the door, he picks up the receiver and dials. He taps his finger rapidly on the desk as it rings.

"Hello?" a man answers.

"Hi, Dr. Jones. Dr. Steen here. You know the project we were talking about a few months ago?"

"Yes, I remember..."

"I may have found a subject for us to use. Is there any way you can come down to my office today?"

"Yes, I can be there within a half hour."

"Great I'll see you then. Bye," Dr. Steen grins.

Hanging up the receiver, he opens Annabelle's file and glances over the half page of information.

"Oh, my dear Annabelle. If you are from where you say you are, you are going to make us famous."

A knock on the door a while later interrupts him. He closes the file quickly before shouting, "Come in!"

A nurse brings in a man and leaves, looking suspicious.

"Great to see you, Dr. Jones. Please, have a seat. Let me tell you about this girl, she's amazing. She's dressed in 1940s clothes, and actually believes it's 1945. I know you have connections in the University, and I'm limited with what I can do here. If you can get the equipment to conduct the tests, we could determine if she is really from 1945. You and I may have just found a way to cement our reputations in gold! But first, we have to get her out of here."

"I can get my hands on all the equipment," Dr. Jones smiles cunningly. "The problem is where to conduct the tests. I cannot rent one of the buildings myself, but if you can rent the building, I'm game."

"I'll get one of those buildings rented!"

"There is one more thing, Dr. Steen. I would like to see this specimen first."

Both men stand up and walk to the ward where Annabelle was being held. Dr. Steen opened the door to Annabelle's room, and Dr. Jones quickly made his way over to the sleeping patient. He almost drools looking at her in amazement. Reaching down and touching her shirt, he turns to Dr. Steen.

"Absolutely amazing. This material is heavy, and the way it's made is absolutely authentic to the 1940s. And she's so young. She can't be more than 17 years old. Fantastic! I could honestly say she is from 1945 at least. If we can prove the theory of a fountain of youth and time travel, we will definitely be beyond rich."

"Excellent!" Dr. Steen smiles. "I can have the paperwork for her release in 20 minutes, but we will need a van to transport her out here in."

Dr. Jones looks thoughtful for a few moments. "I'll provide the van. I know the university has one facility available immediately. If you can get that booked and rented, we should be able to get her out of here within a day or two."

"I'll have the building rented by tomorrow morning. I'll have the forms for her release ready and waiting in my office."

"Sounds like a plan. Absolutely extraordinary. I look forward to seeing what makes her tick."

"I'll be right back, I forgot something in my office," Dr. Steen replies, hurrying out of the room.

Shortly after, a nurse comes into Annabelle's room.

"Excuse me, but what are you doing in here?"

"I'm Dr. Jones. I was just checking on Annabelle for Dr. Steen."

The nurse checks her clipboard, glaring up at Dr. Jones as she asks, "You're not on the list. Tell me, what you really are doing here?"

"I'm here on Dr. Steen's orders. We were discussing transferring her to a new facility."

The nurse gives Dr. Jones a suspicious stare, but before she can say something, Dr. Steen returns.

"I've got this, nurse. You can go about your rounds," he says loudly from the doorway.

The nurse continues to give both of them a dirty look as she walks away.

"That was close," Dr. Steen sighs, looking out the door. "Did she ask you a lot of questions?"

Dr. Jones shakes his head slightly, "No, just basic questions like what I was doing here. I better get going though, I have a lot of work to prep for."

The two men shake hands and go their separate ways.

Walking back to his office, Dr. Steen looks around excited but nervous at the same time. Once he gets into his office, he sits at his desk and picks up the phone. He dials 555-1824, the phone begins to ring, and Robbie picks up.

"Hello?" he answers.

"Hello, Robbie? I need a favor of you. I need you to rent a building at the University for me. No one must know about this except for you and me, all right?"

"I don't have that kind of money, Doctor. I..." he hesitates.

"Don't worry about the money, I'll bring you the deposit and a couple months in advance rent. I'll even throw in an extra 500 bucks for you, but you have to rent it tomorrow and get the keys."

"Okay, where would you like to meet?"

"How about we meet for lunch at McDonald's. Around noon tomorrow?"

"I'll see you then, doctor."

Dr. Steen hangs up the phone and bangs his desk excitedly as this plan comes together.

July 17, 2000: 9:03 AM

Dr. Steen headed into Annabelle's room carrying a notebook. He sat beside the bed, and Annabelle glared at him with hate filled eyes.

"Good morning, Annabelle. How are we feeling today?"

Annabelle continues to glare at him as she answered with hostility. "I want to get out of here. You have no right to hold me here against my will."

"I'm sorry, Annabelle, but we have to do tests on you before we can let you go. These tests won't take too long…"

A police officer came into the room coughing, interrupting the doctor.

"Excuse me, doctor. Can I speak with Annabelle for a moment alone?"

"Fine. Make it quick," Dr. Steen snapped.

The officer nods and sits down beside Annabelle.

"I'm sorry I didn't believe you, Annabelle. I did look into your name. I don't believe in this time travel stuff but I found you in the missing person's database. I'm actually still not sure what's going on. Your missing picture looks almost exactly like you do right now. Seems you disappeared July 16, 1945. Your purse was found in the cemetery by the grave of Raymond Church. Can you tell me the items that were in your purse?"

Annabelle's glare starts to fade as she answered, "I had my brush, my wallet containing $14 and some change, and the scarf my mother bought for me. Does this mean I can get out of here now?"

"I can't get you out of here yet. There's a 72 hour hold to check your mental status. I will fight to try to get you out sooner, but all I can do right now is apologize for not doing my job. As for your items, they're in our storage room at the police station."

Annabelle looked worried as she watched the doctor peeking at her through the open door.

"I don't trust that doctor. Please get me out of this place, I can't stand being tied to this bed any longer."

"I'll do what I can to get you out of here. I'll start working on your case right away."

"Please, make it quick!"

***

Dr. Steen came into McDonald's just after noon. Looking around, he watched out for Robbie. Seeing him in the back corner, he makes his way over, handing him an envelope and sitting down.

"There's $2,400 in this envelope. I called earlier and building 284 is available. Make sure you get that signed, sealed, and delivered by 4 PM."

"I'll call as soon as the deal is done."

Dr. Steen stood up and reached into his pocket, pulling out $500 and slapping it in front of Robbie. "Don't let me down."

Robbie nods as he stands up and shakes Dr. Steen's hand before leaving.

Back at the office, Dr. Steen sits waiting impatiently for the call. It's 2:37 PM when his phone rings. He quickly grabs the receiver before the first ring finishes.

"Hello?"

"Dr. Steen? You have yourself a building. Should I drop the keys off for you?"

"Can I reach you at this number? I'll give you a call in five minutes."

"Yes, you can reach me here. I'll be waiting for your call."

"Great I'll call you soon."

Dr. Steen hangs up and picks up the receiver again, this time calling Dr. Jones.

"Hello Dr. Steen! I presume our little venture is a go?"

"Yes, the building is rented, but I'll need you to pick up the keys. I'll give you the number and you can arrange it. The number is 555-1131."

"Alright, I'll give him a call right away. I'll be there around four to pick up Annabelle."

"Great! I'll make sure she's sedated before you come."

"Sounds good, I'll see you then."

Dr. Steen hangs up, sits back in his chair, and revels in his victory. While sitting there, sipping his coffee, he watches the clock like a hawk. As 3:30 approaches, he gets up to make his rounds to

Annabelle with a loaded syringe in his pocket. As he passes the head nurse, Zelda, she stops him.

"Excuse me. Dr. Steen? I have been meaning to ask you this morning about the man who was here yesterday. Why was he looking at Annabelle?"

"He's a friend of mine. I wanted a second opinion about something, that's all!"

4:15 PM

A white cargo van pulls up to the front doors of the psychiatric center and Dr. Jones gets out with another man. They open the back door and pull out a stretcher, walking in the front doors to the desk where nurse Zelda looks up at them. Dr. Jones hands nurse Zelda a form and looks around nervously.

"Sure is warm one out there today," he says.

Nurse Zelda glares at him as she looks over the paperwork. "Can I ask why she's being transferred? I thought she was going to be released on the 19th?"

Dr. Jones looked surprised and fumbled for an answer. "I'm not sure exactly why. I was just told to come pick her up and transfer her to a new facility."

"Just wait here a moment, I'm going to go get Dr. Steen."

A few minutes after, Zelda returns with Dr. Steen.

"I'm sorry for disrupting you. It seems Zelda has been overworked lately and didn't see that I signed off on her transfer. Go ahead and head down to room 114!"

July 18, 2000

As Annabelle lays in a chemically induced coma, Dr. Jones and his team begin their invasive tests. Jeremy brings a tray over to the metal table where Dr. Jones is filling a fourth vile with Annabelle's blood. Andrew grabs a scalpel and makes a one-inch slit in Annabelle's left leg and places another device inside. He keeps pushing until he hits her femur and a grinding sound emanates from her leg as he twists the metal bar. Thirty seconds later, he pulls it out and places a bone marrow sample in a stainless-steel dish.

"Looks like you got a really good sample there," Dr. Jones says.

"Yes, and healthy too. This woman actually volunteered to have all these tests done on her?" Andrew asks.

Dr. Jones nods as he places the last vile in a styrofoam case. "Yes, I was shocked as well when she signed the forms."

"She impressed me. I mean all the tests she has coming, she'll be lucky if she's walking again in six months."

Dr. Jones nods while he makes an incision in Annabelle's abdomen. He inserts a clear hose into Annabelle's stomach. As he squeezes, fluid comes up the hose and into the beaker. Once the beaker is half full, he quits. David comes over from the other side of the room and takes the beaker away.

"Dr. Jones, her pressures dropping. We should conclude the tests for today," Sally says.

"Yes, we'll have to conclude the tests for today. We will begin again first thing tomorrow morning."

Everyone helps with cleaning up Annabelle, placing gauze and bandages over the multiple surgery sites. David wheels over a camera that will sit above Annabelle until they begin again tomorrow morning.

Dr. Jones walks into the monitoring room where Andrew is logging in his information.

"Annabelle didn't sign up for this, Dr. Jones. There is no way anyone would agree to go through this."

Dr. Jones closes the door, and looks at Andrew. "What makes you say that? She signed up for this to be done to her in the name of science and humanity. Don't start filling people's heads with false information, or you'll be off this team. Everything is signed in triplicate and this is documented in the University's research office."

"Let's say she did sign up for this. Shouldn't we take these tests a lot slower than we are? I mean, we almost lost her once. I don't think she signed up for that."

"Andrew, we have a limited amount of time to do these tests. Everything we're doing is costing millions of dollars. If we slow down, it'll cost more. Just concentrate on your job and I'll concentrate on mine. The sooner we get these tests done, the sooner Annabelle will have her life back."

"With all the tests that we are going to be doing, will Annabelle even have a life to live? The surgery I have scheduled for her tomorrow evening... I'm going to be taking multiple grafts of her muscles. Even at the best of times healing takes eight weeks, and that's before she's able to move those muscles again properly. If you add the surgeries that still need to be conducted after that, she may not even be able to walk again."

"Andrew, get off it," Dr. Jones yells, slamming his hand on the table. "We are going to do the tests she agreed to. I don't give a rat's ass what you think. Now, you have a choice. Either you go according to the documents you signed, or we'll rip them up and you go on your way."

"I'll stay. But I will not be responsible for what happens to that girl. Whatever happens to her will be on your conscience."

"Everything's always on my head. Do your job and everything will be just fine."

Dr. Jones gets up, and slams the door on his way out. Andrew turns and watches Annabelle on the monitor, wondering what Dr. Jones is really up to? After making sure the doctor has left, he picks up the phone and dials the research office.

July 18, 2000

Dr. Steen is in his office, talking on the phone to Dr. Jones.

"The tests on her blood will be back in a week? How come? They should be back within 3 to 4 days. I see. I'll call you right back, someone's at my door. Come in!"

Nurse Zelda walks in, followed by Officer Reese.

"Dr. Steen? Officer Reese is here to see you. I'll wait outside."

"What can I do for you today, officer?"

Officer Reese hands Dr. Steen a paper and responds, "I'm here to pick up Annabelle Church. I made a big mistake by bringing her here. She isn't insane."

"I'm sorry officer, but I can't release her. Not yet anyways. You see, she's been sedated. Perhaps she'll be ready if you come back tomorrow."

"I'll be here at 9 AM. Have her ready."

Dr. Steen watches as the officer turns and walks away. He quickly closes the door and runs back to his phone. He dials Dr. Jones' number, but there's no answer. Pacing around his office, Dr. Steen quickly realizes the severity of his predicament. After several more attempts to call Dr. Jones, he decides to take a drive down to the University himself.

Walking into the facility, Dr. Steen is amazed at all the high-tech equipment surrounding him. As his footsteps echo across the cement floor, he is met by Andrew.

"What are you doing here, doctor? This is a restricted area. I'll have to ask that you leave right away."

"It's alright Andrew," shouts Dr. Jones. "He's with me. You can go back to whatever you were doing."

Andrew glares as he heads back to the monitoring room while Dr. Steen and Dr. Jones head over to Annabelle's bed. Andrew sits down and goes back to watching Annabelle, turning up the volume on the microphone.

"…this is barely scratching the surface of the tests we have planned for Annabelle. Tomorrow we will be going even deeper. Once we get her blood back from testing, this will tell us how she stayed youthful for 55 years. We have a world of tools at our disposal, and if by chance we do lose her…?" Dr. Jones says.

"I need Annabelle ready to go tomorrow morning at 9. The police officer who brought her in is discharging her and there's nothing I can do about it," Dr. Steen interrupts.

"I have spent $2 million on this room full of equipment, and now you tell me I have wasted it. You better come up with something convincing to tell that officer, because it'll be a cold day in hell before I give up this gift. I don't care if you have to commit the officer for psychiatric evaluation, or if you have to shoot him dead. Annabelle is going to stay here until we discover her secrets. Do you understand, Dr. Steen?"

"You can't be serious, Dr. Jones. How do you expect me to kill an officer or get him committed? There has to be another way."

"Look here. I need three days. At least by then we should have the majority of the tests done... if we work her 24 hours straight. If she dies, we'll put her back in the hospital and say she passed away. That's the best I can do for you."

Andrew is horrified as he listens to the conversation continue. Getting up, he quickly makes his way out of the building. Dr. Jones and Dr. Steen follow, seeing the expression on his face, but soon lose him in the darkness.

"Dammit! I forgot about the microphone on the camera. I bet that son of a bitch heard everything we just said. Looks like we have another problem to take care of," sighs Dr. Jones.

"What if he goes to the cops? We'll both be ruined."

"Don't worry, Steen, he won't go to the police. He wouldn't be that stupid. The documents he signed ensure full disclosure. Just go home. I'll figure this out myself.

July 19, 2000

Officer Reese makes his way into the psychiatric center and stops at the front desk. Nurse Zelda greets him with a smile.

"Hi. I'm here to pick up Annabelle Church? I talked to Dr. Steen yesterday and he said she would be ready to go."

Nurse Zelda looks confused as she answers, "Annabelle Church is no longer here. She was transferred out on the 17th I believe. Give me one second to check the files here."

"Dr. Steen didn't mention anything about Annabelle being transferred. What's going on here?"

"The file isn't here," she responds, sifting through papers. "Let me page Dr. Steen. He'll know what's going on?"

A moment later, Dr. Steen walks in.

"I'm a busy man, what do you wa…? Oh, I'm sorry officer. What can I do for you?"

"Why was Annabelle Church transferred?" officer Reese asks.

"We had no choice, officer. She was too out of control for us to deal with! She will be ready to go tomorrow, I've already arranged for her release. I must get going now."

"No, Dr. Steen. Annabelle Church is to be released this morning. I gave you the paperwork yesterday. If she is not out here, I'm placing you under arrest."

"How dare you. On what grounds do you figure you can arrest me?"

Ofc. Reese reaches for his handcuffs and walks over to Dr. Steen, grabbing him by the arm. "You're under arrest for the unlawful confinement of a minor! Give me your other arm."

Dr. Steen willingly puts his arms behind his back as he answers, "You have no right to arrest me. I've done nothing wrong."

Officer Reese turns him around so he's looking into his eyes. "Where is she being held?"

Dr. Steen looks worried as he stares Officer Reese in the eyes.

"Wait! Dr. Jones. He was one of the ones that came to take Annabelle. I'm just not sure where they would've taken her?" Nurse Zelda interjects.

"Who is this Dr. Jones, and where is Annabelle?"

Dr. Steen refuses to say another word while nurse Zelda busies herself, trying to find the paperwork.

July 19, 2000

Forgotten Past

Being called back to the facility by Dr. Jones, Andrew makes his way up the barely lit walkway. Looking around worried, he opens the door and heads inside. His footsteps echo and the door slams behind him. Andrew makes his way to the monitoring room, and sits down, staring at the screen. He looks at the clock, knowing he's a half hour early. Fifteen minutes later, and the door slams shut again. Looking out the window, Andrew sees Dr. Jones walking quickly towards the monitoring room.

"Oh, Andrew. You're here already. I wasn't expecting you for another 15 minutes."

"I figured I'd finish up business I had earlier. What did you want to talk to me about, Dr. Jones?"

Dr. Jones crosses his arms as he glares at Andrew curiously. He paces back and forth in a short line, huffing.

"I'll tell you, Andrew. After yesterday's outburst, you are being removed from this program. I cannot have people working for me who do not believe in what we are trying to accomplish. You just don't understand the opportunity for a better future."

"Are you serious, Dr. Jones? You're willing to kill an innocent teenager over some misguided belief? The tests you did today alone were brutal! She died five times on that very table. You put her through what no human body is capable of, and you did it with a smile on your face. And after what I heard between you and Dr. Steen last night..."

Dr. Jones pushes Andrew back into the chair as he screams, "Don't tell me what to do, Andrew! What you heard between Dr. Steen and myself is confidential, and you had no right to listen in. Annabelle signed up for this. She knew the risks that were involved. Yes, she died five times, but we are on an extremely tight schedule. We are spending millions of dollars on these tests. Perhaps you would like to fund this operation? No, of course you wouldn't, because then you'd be playing with your money and not mine."

Andrew pushes Dr. Jones's arm away and stands up, glaring into his eyes. "You don't have her permission to do any of these tests. I checked with the research office, and there is no Annabelle Church on file. You kidnapped her from the psychiatric center for your own ungodly needs. Just confess what you did to that girl."

Dr. Jones pushes Andrew back, and reaches into his jacket, pulling out a pistol. Pointing it at Andrew, he smiles gleefully. "Well, Andrew? You want to know the whole story? Fine. Annabelle Church is a special girl. Imagine breaking the dimensional barriers of time and space. 1945 to 2000. A sixteen-year-old girl is still sixteen. What do you know about 1945, Andrew?"

Forgotten Past

"I know what I've read in books. Even if she is from 1945, how does this give you any right to conduct horrific tests that will probably kill her?"

"Oh, shut up. Yes, there is a good possibility she will end up dead, but so what? She doesn't belong here anyway. Who's going to miss her? You? Her family? They're probably long gone. They've probably forgotten about her years ago. You don't see the future in this, and I suspect you never will. After I take care of you, you will be no more than a forgotten memory."

"Perhaps you can rejoice in murder, but I highly doubt you'll rejoice in anything else," Andrew yells back.

"Perhaps you're right, Andrew. But then again, who cares? I'll be rich and you'll be dead. Goodbye."

Dr. Jones raises the gun so it's pointing straight at Andrew's head, but a voice interrupts him.

"Drop that gun, Dr. Jones!"

A police officer holds his gun to Dr. Jones's head as he steps out from the back room. Dr. Jones raises his hands, glaring at Andrew.

"You called the cops? You know what you've done now, right? You've set all of humanity back at least 20 years. I should have shot you as soon as I walked in."

The officer handcuffs Dr. Jones as the medical staff attend to Annabelle. Officers escort him out, as the first officer kneels in front of Andrew.

"Are you okay, Andrew? I know that was pretty harrowing, but you put a serious villain in jail. There's no way either Dr. Steen or Dr. Jones will ever see the light of day again."

"I'm sorry I was a part of this. I never wanted to hurt anyone, especially not someone so young and innocent. When Annabelle wakes up, could you apologize to her for me? I deserve to be in jail with them. I did a few procedures on her myself."

"You can tell her yourself when you see her in the hospital. Without you and nurse Zelda, we would never have known what happened to Annabelle. You saved her life, don't take that away from yourself."

July 26, 2000

Lying in a hospital bed, Annabelle looks at her arms in disgust. She had woken up this morning in discomfort. She could see signs of her surgeries, but had no idea where they had come from. After an hour of checking herself out, a nurse finally came in to check on her.

"How are you feeling today, Annabelle?"

"What happened to me? Where'd all these stitches and bruises come from?"

"I'll get the doctor to come and explain what happened."

She walked out of the room, leaving Annabelle staring at the door. Within moments a doctor walked in, smiling.

"Good morning, Annabelle. I want you to know you are going to be fine. I can't go into full details of what happened to you, but what I can tell you is that these wounds will heal and you'll be back to normal."

"I want to know what happened to me," Annabelle replies angrily, looking at her injuries. "What was done to me? Who did this, and what did they do it for?"

The doctor looked unsure of what to say as he stood there looking at his clipboard. He sighed. "Okay. To be honest, I don't know what all they did to you in that facility. I know they experimented on you, but I don't know exactly what they did. The most I could do is speculate."

"What the hell do you mean they experimented on me? What facility are we talking about? What the hell did you guys do to me? I want out of here right now!"

The doctor stops Annabelle from getting up out of bed, and she scratches him across the face.

"Someone get in here!" he shouts.

Annabelle continues to scratch and punch at the doctor as he tries to protect his face. Two nurses come running in and grab Annabelle, pushing her back down onto the bed. Annabelle screams and fights as they place her arms in restraints, and then her feet. One gives Annabelle a needle in the arm, and shortly after she is sedated.

"What did you do?" one of the nurses asks.

Wiping the blood off his cheek, he replies, "I told her what the police told me I could tell her. I don't know what made her flip out like that?"

Their conversation was cut short by a page over the intercom. "Dr. Saber to the emergency room. Stat!"

The doctor and nurses make their way to the emergency room. As they arrive, they stop dead in their tracks, facing 50 or so people.

"We've already called in all off-duty staff," a triage nurse explains. "We're overrun with patients here. They all have flu-like symptoms and the worst ones are exhibiting signs of pneumonia. The one patient is a police officer. His name is Vincent Reece and he's in exam room 12."

Dr. Saber grabs the clipboard from the triage nurse. "Reese? Isn't he the one that brought Annabelle in?"

"I'm not sure, but you best get into the exam room and take a look at him. I don't think he's going to last much longer."

Dr. Saber looks worried as he hurriedly goes to exam room 12. Opening the door, the clipboard drops from his hand as he stands there looking at Officer Reese.

"I've never seen anything like it, have you Dr. Sabre?" the nurse asks, coming in behind him.

He stares at the officer's face. It's covered with red blotches, some of which are oozing pus. Turning towards the nurse, trying to hold his breakfast down, he asks, "What does he have? Measles?"

"I don't know, Dr. Saber. Apparently, the red blotches appeared about two hours ago. The officer that brought in this man said he'd been coughing pretty good the last week. We've already taken a blood sample, and he's been given a morphine shot to ease the pain."

Dr. Saber nods as he turns to look towards Officer Reese. Walking over to him, he unbuttons his shirt to take a closer look. He jumps back fearfully as he notices the lymph nodes ready to burst. Vincent begins coughing uncontrollably and blood spurts out with each cough. He gasps for air as he grabs the rails of his bed. Within a minute, he lets out one last gasp of air as the monitor flat lines.

"Get the crush cart in here immediately!" the nurse yells.

Dr. Saber shakes his head as he responds sorrowfully, "there's no need. I think the most humane thing we can do for him is let him rest in peace."

"I hope this isn't going to be your opinion of the other ones."

Dr. Saber turns towards the nurse with wide eyes. "You're telling me there are more people out there that have the same thing?"

"Every one of them. They are all in various stages of this unknown pathogen."

Dr. Saber hurries over to the door and looks out into the waiting room with fear in his eyes. There are men, women, and children coughing.

July 27, 2000

Annabelle sits with Ann Dumont, the hospital psychiatrist, in frustrating silence.

"Now Annabelle, please tell me what happened to you. From the beginning?"

"You tell me. I'm sure you know more than I do."

"Annabelle, if we are going to get anywhere, you're going to have to open up to me. Now, please tell me what you remember since you came here."

Annabelle continues to glare as she answers, "I came through between two trees in the cemetery. I had a police officer harass me, then he took me to a hospital where apparently some doctors decided to try and dissect me. Now I'm sitting here talking to you. Anything else you want to know?"

"I know this is difficult for you. I want to help you in every way I can. Please let me."

Annabelle looks her dead in the eyes while she answers,

"You want to help me? Really help me? Then get me the hell out of this stink hole. All I want is to go home and be with my family again. Can you do that for me, doctor?"

"I'm sorry, but I can't release you until you're healed. As a doctor, that would be irresponsible of me to let you go. Let's just get you better, okay?"

Annabelle mutters something under her breath as she stands up. She glares at the doctor, "I am healed, Dr. Dumont. I'm going back to my room because I have nothing more to say to you."

Annabelle storms out of the doctor's office as Dr. Dumont follows closely behind. Annabelle falls on the floor on the way back to her room. She lies there, holding her left leg, as Dr. Dumont and another nurse come running.

"Stay away from me!" she shouts, angrily.

Dr. Dumont stops nearby as the nurse helps Annabelle to her feet. Annabelle begins limping away.

"Please Annabelle, let me help you," Dr. Dumont calls after her.

Annabelle stops, leans against the wall, and turns to look at Dr. Dumont.

"Help me?" she howls. "I think you and your friends have done enough to me."

Dr. Dumont stands there, dumbfounded, as she looks at the hatred spewing out of Annabelle's eyes. Annabelle continues to limp towards her room with the nurse following close behind. The nurse helps Annabelle lay back in her bed, and checks to see if any of the stitches have reopened.

"All nursing staff to room 201," a voice crackles over the loudspeaker.

In room 201, Dr. Florence stands at the front of the room. She looks at the nursing staff as she exclaims sadly,

"As you all know, we've had an unknown pathogen wreak havoc on this, and other, hospitals. Right now, the death toll is under 100, but that could change quickly. Everyone is working on trying to figure out what it is, but we are still unsure of how long the incubation period is. What we do know from Vincent Reece, the first victim yesterday, is that once the symptoms are full-blown, death is usually within a few hours. It seems Vincent had a cold or flu for the last week, but we cannot be sure of this. It gives us a timeline of the 18th – 20th. We also believe this may be airborne, but we can't be sure until the tests come back."

A nurse near the front quickly asks, "If it's airborne, should we all be tested?"

Dr. Florence nods as she answers coldly, "Honestly, if it's airborne, no test is going to come back fast enough. That is why from right now until we start getting tests back, everyone is confined to the hospital."

The room begins to grumble as everyone shouts at Dr. Florence, but one question makes it to Dr. Florence's ears,

"Where did the pathogen come from? Surely, it's something we know about it? After all, this isn't the dark ages of medicine. With the technology, it should give us some idea of what we're dealing with."

"We do know something about this pathogen, but the problem is the components of this virus. I'll make it short and sweet. You know how the cold virus works. The incubation period is relatively quick, and over even quicker. We are looking at viruses that are being resurrected- measles, malaria, influenza, the Black plague- all rolled up into one virus. Like the cold virus, the incubation period is probably within a week. Once it becomes full-blown, the patient will die within hours. Each virus on their own we could kill, but right now nothing is working. I wish I could tell you more, but right now we are on the losing end of this virus. My best suggestion is to do your job and hope we find a cure for this monstrosity."

The room fell silent as everyone looks fearfully at Dr. Florence.

"I'm sorry, but I'm not buying this. I mean, how can viruses that are so different combine into one biological cell?" a nurse asks.

Dr. Florence looks towards the floor, as if she's trying to find an answer in the air. As everyone stares towards her, she finally responds.

"I don't know. Just as you said, it doesn't make sense. I'm sorry I don't have a legitimate answer for any of you. All I can say is, do your job the best you can and let's hope there are no more fatalities."

The room disbands and heads to their workstations, more worried than ever.

July 28, 2000

Annabelle paced around her room as Dr. Dumont looked through the window in the door. Every time she tried to come in, Annabelle threw the chair towards her.

"Annabelle? Please, this isn't helping you. Let's go back to my office and talk?" Dr. Dumont says through the door.

Annabelle stopped pacing and stared at Dr. Dumont, enraged. "You want to help? Find a way to get me home. I'm done dealing with any of you anymore! I just want to get out of here, and go home where I belong."

"I'm trying my best, Annabelle, but unless you help me, I can't get you out of here. Why don't you come with me to my office? We'll sit down, talk, and see what we can do, okay?"

Dr. Dumont opened the door a little more, and Annabelle stormed out of the room with a slight limp.

"I have your best interest at heart, Annabelle. I'm going to try everything I can to get you out of here as quick as possible," Dr. Dumont says, walking alongside her.

Getting to the office, Annabelle sits down, holding her left leg. Dr. Dumont sits down in her chair and looks Annabelle in the eyes.

"I told you everything I remember. I don't know what more you want me to tell you. You want to know what I know? I'll tell you. I miss my mom, my dad, and I miss my life. I don't know why you guys are keeping me locked up here. I haven't done anything, but I've been used like a guinea pig. All you and the doctors care about is keeping me here, but I just want to go."

"Yes, I would feel the same way as you if I were in your position. The doctors that experimented on you had no right to do so. I know they say you are from 1945, but how do we know? Until I can prove or disprove where you are from, I have to keep you here. So, let's start trying to figure out where you're from?"

"Check my birth certificate! Look me up! I was born in 1929. The officer who came to see me in the other hospital. Check with him, he found my purse. He'll know who I am."

Dr. Dumont quickly scribbles down something in the notebook, and replies,

"Okay, I'll check with the police station to see who the officer was. If you go back to your room, I should have an answer for you later today," the doctor responds, scribbling on her notepad.

At the police station, Captain Ricky packs up Officer Reece's items. He places them in a box, one at a time, and grabs a card, looking at it closely.

"Miss Anna Rosin. 306-555-9786. Annabelle Church's sister," he reads.

Slipping the card into his uniform pocket, he packs the remaining items and closes the box. Tears fill his eyes as he walks away. Walking past everyone without saying a word, he makes his way outside to a payphone. Grabbing the card out of his pocket, he dials the number.

After a brief exchange of words, Mrs. Rosin agrees to meet him at the station. Two hours later, she walks in. She has graying brown hair, and a well-aged appearance. Another officer leads her to Captain Ricky's office.

"Why did you want to see me, Captain? You were really vague when I talked to you on the phone?" she asks.

The Captain leaned forward, motioning for her to sit down. Looking somewhat confused himself, he opened Officer Reese's file.

"Yes, and I do apologize about that Mrs. Rosin. One of my officers who recently passed away was working on a case. Did you have a sister named Annabelle Church?"

Mrs. Rosin gives the captain a look and clenched her teeth. "Annabelle? There's a name I haven't heard in a long time. A name I prefer not to hear again! Why are you bringing her up? Did you finally find her bones?"

The captain looked at her worried before answering cautiously, "Your sister Annabelle is alive. After everything she's been through, and seeing that you're her only living family..."

Anna glares as she puts her hand up to stop the captain from speaking.

"Don't you even go there, officer. I have spent a lifetime loathing that name. When I was a young girl, all I ever heard about was Annabelle. Anything I did to please my parents fell on deaf ears. I tried to be a good daughter, but could never meet my parents' expectations of Annabelle. God, you can't even imagine the frustration of living in someone else's shadow. I understand they didn't know if she was murdered or kidnapped, but I just wish they could have loved me like they loved Annabelle. That's all I ever wanted. My parents had a lit candle sitting in the window every day since Annabelle left.

Please don't give me the speech about forgiveness, I lost that a long time ago. My mom buried herself in her baking while my father buried himself in booze. I was an unwanted child. Family gatherings were all about Annabelle. Even in school, everyone talked about Annabelle. I was asked everyday if they had found out anything more about Annabelle's disappearance. What am I supposed to feel? You want me to go see the one person who practically destroyed my life as a child. How can I forgive that?"

The captain looks into Anna's teared up eyes and fiddles his thumbs as he responds, "I'm sorry this happened to you, Anna. Do you really think Annabelle set out to ruin your life as a child?"

"I don't think she purposely set out to do me any harm, but because of her I lost my parents. I lost my parents by the time I was eight years old. I was nothing to them. I tried everything to show them I loved them, and I got nothing back. Please don't ask me to go see her, because I will not."

"Have you ever thought about what Annabelle might be going through? She was torn away from your parents, too. She's frightened and doesn't understand how she got here. Perhaps you should try to put yourself in her shoes for a mile, go through everything she's gone through. She's been here over a week. She's had doctors experimenting on her, and everyone she knows is gone. I understand you had a hard life, but you aren't the only one that's had a pile of shit thrown at their feet. If you'd like, we can go see Annabelle at the hospital. If not, I guess I'll say goodbye."

"You have a good day, Captain Ricky!"

He watches as she walks out of his office.

July 29, 2000

At 7:30 in the morning, as more and more patients flock to the three hospitals, the doctors and nurses continue to fight a losing battle. No bed is ever empty for long, and the ones that do leave the beds, are leaving in body bags. As the momentum of this contagion gains power, the Saskatchewan government is forced to call a state of emergency. Radios and televisions and any plays the same message:

"If you are experiencing a persistent cough, please quarantine yourself from others. This unknown virus is becoming an epidemic. Please seek medical attention at the first signs of cold or flu-like symptoms."

Scientists and biologists with viral knowledge scour over the virus piece by piece. Every time they get close to unlocking a piece of the virus, another piece shuts down the possible cure. Many of the biologists have dubbed the virus the "Rubik's cube" due to the missing pieces.

In the emergency room, Dr. Robbins checks on a patient who arrived that morning. Walking over to her bedside, he examines the red blotches on her face and asks, "Jasmine Smith? Can you hear me?"

"Yes," she nods, answering quietly.

"Can you tell me when you first began feeling ill?"

Jasmine nods as she struggles to bring air into her lungs. "At home," she whispers.

Dr. Robbins quickly scribbles on the notepad as he continues speaking, "Did you come in contact with anything or anyone?"

"Yes, a girl…?"

She brings up blood as she coughs. The doctor helps her move onto her side as blood spurts into a tray. After a few moments, Jasmine is able to breathe again.

"A girl said I was in her house…?"

Dr. Robbins quickly scribbles, but before he can ask her another question, Jasmine is coughing again. He places the oxygen mask over

Jasmine's nose and mouth and she calms down a little bit. Dr. Robbins looks at Jasmine closely, and decides it be better if he left for now. Walking out into the waiting room, he glances at the hundred or more people sitting in pain.

"We're not going to make it, are we Dr. Robbins?" a nurse asks.

"No, I don't believe we are going to make it through this epidemic. I'm already exhibiting the signs. My cough is slowly getting worse, and I feel like I have an elephant on my chest. I'm no closer to knowing what we're dealing with."

"Shouldn't you be laying down then? I'm sure there's another doctor that could take over for you for the time being?"

"There is nobody else. All the other doctors are sick or dead."

"Why weren't we told? We should have been the first to know what was going on," the nurse answers, angry.

"We were told by administration not to say anything as it would bring down morale. I'll stay as long as I can, but considering the progression I've noticed, I should be in one of these beds by the middle of the night."

"Who is going to replace you?"

"You are," Robbins chokes out as he starts coughing.

The nurse quickly grabs Dr. Robbins around the chest as she holds him up. They make their way to an available chair, where she helps him sit down. As he coughs, little splatters of blood appear on the sleeve of his coat.

"Maybe sooner," he gasps.

As his coughing fit grows, the nurse goes to help another woman who has fallen on the floor. Red blotches cover her entire face and she convulses on the floor. The psychologist, Dr. Dumont, quickly makes her way over to the nurse.

"Get the hell out of here! We've got this, just get out of here!" the nurse yells.

Dr. Dumont looks fearful as she turns around and runs back to the elevator. Heading back upstairs to go see Annabelle, she stands in the elevator shaking with fear over what she just witnessed. As the elevator comes to a stop and the doors open, a man stands in front of her.

"Are you all right?" he asks.

"I am, but don't go down to the emergency room."

"I lost my son Andy an hour ago. I just can't figure how he caught this. So much death, where does it stop? Believe me, I'll stay away from there."

Dr. Dumont shakes her head, patting his arm as she quickly makes her way towards Annabelle's room. Just as she heads down the hallway, a police officer stands stops her.

"Leave her be for a while. Her sister is in there with her," he says.

"She has a sister?"

"Yes, it's a long story. Come with me and I'll tell you all about it?"

Dr. Dumont peeks through the window, and sees Annabelle sitting on her bed with her newly found sister in a chair nearby.

Annabelle stares at Anna, confused, as Anna shakes her head, not knowing what to say.

"So… I have a younger sister?" Annabelle asks.

"Yes, you do. I didn't really want to come to see you. Just the sound of your name brought back so many bad memories for me. After a talk with that officer yesterday, your name kept eating away at me so I decided to come see for myself. How the hell did you stay so young?"

"What did I ever do to you?"

Forgotten Past

"Mom and dad! They loved you something fierce. I just wish they would have loved me even a little bit. From as far back as I can remember, mom turned to baking nonstop, and dad found himself in the bottle. I was taking care of them when I was eight. All they ever thought about was you and what happened to you. In the beginning, I wish I would've gotten to know you, but I grew too loathe your name. I know it sounds selfish, but I just wanted someone to love me and care for me. You were the one they wanted, and I was just a reminder. They even named me Anna, short for Annabelle. What happened to you anyway?"

"I'm sorry, Anna. If I could take anything back, I would take back going through those trees and coming here. I hate it here. They are so mean and uncaring. Look at all the scars from the doctors here. They were willing to kill me to find out what secrets I held. All I can remember for sure from July 16 is that I was visiting our uncle's grave and someone, or something, told me I was in danger. Next thing I know, my life is turned into nothing but a wreck. I'm sorry for any pain I've caused you, Anna. I'm truly sorry."

Annabelle stands up and gives Anna a hug as she weeps onto her shoulder. Anna fights her own feelings of hate, and puts her arms around Annabelle.

"Please forgive me, Annabelle. I'm sorry I never even considered what you would be going through. I spent my whole life hating you for what you did. Now I realize you didn't do anything. I blamed you for our parent's deaths and everything else in between."

Annabelle lifts her head and looks Anna in the eyes. "You had every right to hate me. To me, everything changed in an instant but for you, everything was as it should be. I wish I could've known you when you were young, I would never let you live unloved."

"That's all I've ever wanted. I would give anything to go back and relive my childhood again, just knowing what happened here. What happened to you. I know I would feel better if you had been there with me."

"I know I can't turn back what's done, but perhaps I can be part of your future?" Annabelle asks.

"I would like that. I do have a surprise for you, though. You have a niece and nephew. Their names are Jennifer and Dean. My husband died last year."

"Oh, my gosh, really? I can't wait to meet them! Hopefully I can soon, but there seems to be something going on. I'm not sure what's happening, but I've been hearing a lot of people being sent to the emergency room."

"Yes, hopefully I can introduce you to them soon. As for what's happening around town, there seems to be some sort of virus going around. I know a lot of people have been dying from it."

"Is it like the diseases we had going around in the 40s? They were awful killers. I hope you don't get sick with it?"

"Heavens no. We have been lucky so far, but if I believe the television, we might not be lucky for long."

"Perhaps you should go? I would hate to cause you any more pain than I've already done. Just knowing I have a sister is all I need to get out of this place. Just tell me where you live, and I'll come visit you as soon as I get out of here."

Anna nods slowly as she stands. "I live just behind Woodlawn Cemetery. 1512 1st Avenue North. A block away from where we used to live. I'm glad I was able to make peace with you. I love you, Annabelle."

"I love you, too. I'll get out of here soon, and I'll come see you and your family. I am glad you came to see me. I would hate to go through life not knowing the kind of pain I caused. Please know I never meant to hurt anyone?"

Anna smiles as she walks towards the door, "I know that now. I'll make sure everyone knows I have an older sister that looks way younger than I do."

As Anna leaves the room, Annabelle sits back down on the bed, a smile from ear to ear.

July 30, 2000

Annabelle sits in Dr. Dumont's office.

"I hear you have a sister. At least now you won't be alone here. Perhaps you can introduce her to me one of these days."

"What do you mean by that, doctor? I still don't see why you're holding me here. I'm walking better, and the pain has subsided. Why am I still being held here?"

Dr. Dumont leans forward and kindly replies, "I know you are better, Annabelle, but we must keep you here until we feel you are better. Besides, there is a bad virus going around…"

"Are you kidding me? You're keeping me here until you think I'm better? What gives you the right to keep me here? I haven't done anything. I've come to your stupid office every day, and all you ever do is talk. I'm done talking to you or anyone else. I'm leaving?"

Dr. Dumont stands as Annabelle starts walking out of her office. She follows Annabelle down the hall.

"Quit following me? I have nothing left to say to you, so go back to your office and talk to yourself."

Dr. Dumont continues to follow Annabelle down the hall, and the girl turns around to hits Dr. Dumont in the mouth with a hard right.

"I said stay away from me!"

Annabelle stomps off as Dr. Dumont gets back to her feet, holding her jaw. Heading towards the nurse's station, Dr. Dumont realizes she's lost sight of Annabelle.

Annabelle sneaks into the nurse's lounge. Finding some clothing that fit, she changes out of her hospital gown. Annabelle heads around to the back staircase as an announcement comes over the loudspeaker.

"Annabelle Church, report to security immediately!"

Annabelle hurriedly runs down the stairs, favoring her left leg. Opening the door on the main floor, she walks out past hundreds of people coughing and choking in the emergency room. No one seems to notice her as she slips out the door.

A lab technician comes running up to the fourth floor, holding a thick brown envelope. He stops at the desk.

"You look out of breath? Hopefully you didn't run that all the way here?" the nurse asks.

The man nods as he tries to catch his breath, "I had to take the back stairs. I'm supposed to give this to the one in charge of Annabelle Church."

"Doctor, you better get back here," the nurse calls to Dr. Dumont. "I think this envelope is for you?"

"What is that exactly? Are those test results?" the doctor asks.

"Yes, I was told to bring them to whoever's in charge of Annabelle Church. I have to get back to the lab."

"Thank you!" she says, pulling the papers out. "Oh my God, Brad! We have to find Annabelle. Now."

"We searched the whole floor already, and she isn't up here. Is something wrong that I should know about, doctor?"

"Yes, it appears Annabelle is the carrier of this virus. Call the police and everyone else who is able to search for her."

The nurse quickly gets on the phone, as Dr. Dumont runs down the hall. Within twenty minutes, over a hundred people are searching the hospital for Annabelle. Dr. Dumont speaks with the police captain as everyone searches.

"Officer, do you have any ideas where Annabelle would go? I know she has family now, would you be able to find out where they live?"

Capt. Ricky pulls out his notepad and replies, "yes, I'll get a couple of officers to head over there right now."

In the emergency room, the news anchor on the TV is giving a report on the virus:

"As of 7:03 AM this morning, the government has announced that this new virus, dubbed the Rubik's cube, is being upped in classification to a pandemic from an epidemic. Reports are coming in from all over the globe of people dying of the same virus. Our only hope resides with the many scientists and biologists who are frantically trying to find a cure before it's too late. The Government of Saskatchewan, and Canada have ordered emergency actions in all the provinces. No one will be allowed to travel out of their hometowns. Our thoughts and prayers are with those who need it the most. And now, back to our regularly scheduled program…"

Officers begin searching the surrounding areas in hopes of finding Annabelle nearby while Captain Ricky and a few other officers drive over to Anna's house.

Trying to stay hidden, Annabelle creeps down alleys and snakes her way through the streets. Once she makes it to 33rd Street, she tries to hide in the various yards along the way. Noticing police cars blocking Warman Road, she knows the police are slowly closing in on her. She tries to get as close to the cemetery as possible, and after a few hours of waiting, she can see it maybe a hundred yards away.

"Annabelle Church? Stand up slowly," a man's voice calls out from behind her.

Looking out of the corner of her eye, she slowly turns towards the officer. He walks over with handcuffs. Anger grows in Annabelle's eyes as he grabs her right arm and brings it down. As he does this, Annabelle lets him have it with her left. He lets go of her arm and tries to subdue her, but Annabelle continues to fight, kneeing him in the groin a few times. Knowing she's fighting for her life, she continues the barrage of hits.

She gets away from the officer, and he grabs his radio. Annabelle runs with fury as she crosses Warman road. Climbing the wall of the cemetery, the officer yells at her to stop. She knows the police will catch her quickly. Out of breath, she fights to get to Anna's house. Nearing halfway through the cemetery, a black mist forms in front of her and she stops dead in her tracks, breathing heavily. The shadow floats towards her.

"Annabelle, your time is done here. I'm going to send you back home to your family," it whispers.

"Why did you bring me here anyway..."

The shadow stops Annabelle from speaking, as he states sternly, "Everyone has a journey in life, and this journey is over for you. You can go home now."

"Can you please tell me why I was brought here in the first place?"

"I saved your life from an inevitable death in return for a favor. I sent you to a place where caring for others is low on the list of priorities."

"But why? They did horrible things to me here. Unforgivable things!"

"I know. I gave them one last chance to be better humans, but sadly it wasn't meant to be. So, you gave them a reason to care again. You brought a virus with no cure. Had they not done such horrible things to you, but welcomed you with open arms, none of this would be happening right now."

As Annabelle walked alongside the shadowy mist, she covered her mouth, fearful of what she had done. As she tried to find the words to express how she feels, he continues whispering.

"Don't blame yourself for anything here, it was them who sealed their fate. You were simply a messenger and they chose to mutilate a gift of time. When you go home, you will remember what you've done here. Don't be sad about this though, you'll continue to teach the world how to be a decent person. With your care and love of others, you may be able to change the future."

The mist and Annabelle stand at the two trees she came through. Annabelle sees the police officers coming towards her, shouting.

"What do you mean decent person? How am I supposed to change the whole world?"

"Don't sell yourself short, Annabelle. I have watched you from the cemetery for years. You've been kind to everyone around you, and you have never wronged someone. I know it doesn't seem like it right now, but everything will be as it was when you go back home. Now, walk through these trees and you will be reunited with your family."

"I hope I really am going home. I don't want to deal with these people anymore."

Forgotten Past

The shadow man motions for her to walk as he whispers, "You will be home with your family, I promise. Now, go. Walk to your past…"

Annabelle quickly walks in between the trees as his voice continues to emanate all around her, "…remember, go straight home. I have sent you back five minutes before you saw me. Do not waste time. Go straight home."

Annabelle comes out the other side of the trees, and sees her purse beside Uncle Raymond's grave. Seeing the men coming along the path, she places a kiss on her uncle's headstone and grabs her purse. Quickly making her way out of the cemetery, she runs up the street to her house.

"Annabelle? Slow down!" her mother exclaims.

Annabelle stops as she hears her mother's voice, and a smile grows on her face as she heads into the kitchen. Her mother stands by the sink, and Annabelle runs over to give her a hug.

"What's wrong Annabelle?" her mom asks.

Annabelle just squeezes her tightly as she responds excitedly, "Nothing now! I'm just happy to be home."

"There is something different about you. Did something happen to you when you were visiting Uncle Raymond's grave?"

"Yes, but it's a long story?"

Annabelle motions for her mom to sit down, and Annabelle sits next to her. "Okay, you're going to think I'm crazy…"

When Annabelle finishes recounting her tale, her mom looks puzzled.

"Wait, you're telling me you went into the future? Annabelle, you do realize it's not possible to go 55 years into the future. And you're telling me you went there in an hour?"

"Yes, and everything was so strange there. There was someone else living in our house, and I even learned I have a sister. You and dad named her Anna after I disappeared."

"A sister? How old is she?"

"54," Annabelle grins. "She's born in February of next year. She hated me because I disappeared, and all you and dad could think about was me. We made up though, and she even invited me over to her house."

"Annabelle, I don't know what happened, and I'm sure I don't want to know, but there's no way you could know I'm pregnant.

Whatever you do, do not tell your father. I was going to save that for our anniversary next month."

"I won't tell dad anything, I promise."

Annabelle's mom rubs her forehead, frustrated, as she stares at her daughter in disbelief.

"How about you and I go do some clothes shopping. We'll get something new and spiffy."

"Yes! I'm just going wash up first, okay?"

Annabelle's mother's smiles as she watches Annabelle quickly run up the stairs.

"How the heck did she know I was pregnant?" she mutters to herself. "There's no way she could have known. How did she know what I was going to name the baby Anna if it was a girl? No, this is crazy. She must be assuming. She has to be…"

Annabelle comes running down the stairs in a white dress and lifts her dress up on the left side.

"Look! I still have one of the scars from the experiments they conducted on me in the future."

Annabelle's mom looks closely at the scar, running her fingers over the indent as she answers frightened, "Oh my Lord! You're not lying."

July 31, 2000

The growing pandemic accelerates quicker than any plague known to man. Dr. Dumont stumbles around, the red blotches on her face prominent. A shadowy dark man appears out of nowhere, and Dr. Dumont falls against the wall.

"Who are you?"

The dark shadow steps closer, and kneels down in front of her. He grins coldly as he states, "I am your fate. I gave you a chance for redemption. You had a chance with Annabelle. A chance to show kindness to a stranger from a different time. Instead, you caused her pain and heartache. Your greed to know everything is your downfall. She was your savior from my wrath. The moment you tried to kill her, was the moment you killed yourselves."

Dr. Dumont reaches for the shadow as he stands up and walks down the hall slowly.

"Please, stop this before it's too late?" she tries to call after him.

"Stop? Your fate was sealed the moment those doctors put the needle into Annabelle. That was the moment you released death on yourselves."

The shadow turned and walked away, disappearing into thin air. Only a few minutes pass before Dr. Dumont succumbs to the virus.

July 16, 1955

Annabelle holds Anna's hand as they make their way to the grave of their uncle Raymond. Anna smiles cheerfully as she looks up at Annabelle. Stopping at the grave, Anna kneels on the one side while Annabelle kneels on the other side. Together they clean the debris off the headstone.

"How come we're cleaning off this headstone?" Anna asks.

"Respect. Uncle Raymond fought in the war and he died so everyone could be free. So, we clean up around his grave to show him that we respect what he died for."

Anna smiles as she continues to pick up some leaves. Annabelle looks around worried, as a strange but familiar feeling takes hold. Slowly turning her head towards the two trees, she sees the dark shadow standing there. Annabelle motions for Anna to stay, as she stands up and slowly makes her way over.

"Hello Annabelle," it whispers. "It's been a while since I last saw you. How are things going with your sister?"

"Yes, it's been quite a while? Anna is my best friend. Why are you here?"

"I'm just checking to see how you're doing, and I've come to let you know that the virus overwhelmed the world."

"You mean what I was carrying killed everyone?"

The shadow nods.

"Is it because they wouldn't let me leave?"

"They died because of what they did to you. If they had only been kind instead of monsters. They got what they deserved, and now you have what you deserve. I want you to live every day like it's your last. Enjoy those around you, especially the ones that add meaning to your life. Hold on to them as long as you can, because one day everything could go away in the blink of an eye."

"Yes, I do cherish every moment I have with my sister, and my mom and dad."

"Good. I must go now, but keep adding people to your heart. You are the only person who can save the world. Take care, Annabelle."

The shadow vanishes, and Annabelle turns to walk back to Anna.

"I finished," she says. "Do you think Uncle Raymond likes what I did?"

Annabelle smiles as she grabs Anna's hand and responds, "Yes, Anna, he's proud of you. A little bit of respect goes a long way. How about you and I go home and sneak some apple pie?"

Anna smiles as she begins to run towards home with Annabelle close behind.

August 12, 1999

At the age of 70 years old, Annabelle sits at her table with a pen and paper. She looks out the window at the cemetery, as if she's living every moment of that day over and over again. She begins to write:

I write this as my living testament. I've kept everything secret, except for what I told my mom that day when I was 16. I believe she truly did want to believe me, but even I have no idea if I really did go to the future. There are moments in time where someone or something looks familiar, and sometimes I think I'm downright crazy. How could anyone travel so far into the future? I have looked up these names in the phone book, and I've even called some of these places to see if certain people work there. To my surprise they do. I have wanted to talk to these people and confront them about the evil they thrust upon me. Every time I get up the nerve to do something about it, there's always something in the back of my head that tells me I'm crazy.

Anna, my sister, doesn't know how much she changed my life. Even though I don't tell her, I talked to her later on in life and she hated me to no ends. Somehow, I can't see her being able to get that angry. We spent every day together, growing up and learning from each other. I do know that without Anna in my life I would not be the same person. I hope she knows how much I appreciate what she's done for me.

As for my mom and dad, I'm glad that both of them never turned to the bottle for comfort. You were there for Anna and myself every day. I try to think about what it would've been like to live in Anna's shoes without me, and I shudder to think about the anger hate that could grow from a child disappearing from their parents. It's not something I want to even imagine.

For my two daughters, Elise, and Mary, you and your children mean the world to me. I am proud to call you my daughters and my grandchildren. I hope your futures are bright and full of love. I couldn't ask for better family than what I have! Thank you.

Forgotten Past

July 16, 2000 is a day I've been fearing since 1945. I don't know if it was a sneak preview of my own fate, or events to come, but I know the only way I will know positively is when that day comes. If it is my fate to die, I know I lived a long and beautiful life. I have treated people with respect, and have received respect in return. If these events do happen as I saw them, I will die, but there are parts of me that hope it was all a dream. I won't know the truth until July 16, and until then I'll do what I've always done... Live for today.

To anyone who reads this letter, take what you will from it. Each person will read it differently, and that's okay. Difference in opinions is what makes the world turn. Cutting others down for their opinion is what creates disasters. Love each other and be good to each other, because you never know when you may need someone's help. The future is never a promise of a better life. The real question is what will you do when it comes? Will you be there helping others, or helping yourself?

Pankratz

The House God Damned

Prologue

Standing in the front parlor of my newly built house, I look around at everything father added to make it mine. I glance towards the door as my sisters, Jessica and Stephanie, come in.

"How dare you steal Stan from me, you hussy," Stephanie shouts.

"I didn't! He was never interested in you!" I shout back, pushing.

"Liar!" Jessica yells, stepping closer.

Stephanie slaps me across the face with her right hand, as I slap her across her left cheek. "You have to be delusional to believe he was in love with you," I continue.

"You know Stephanie wanted him, you should have left him alone," Jessica bellows.

"Then she should have said something to him!"

"He's mine!" Stephanie whines.

I barely seeing the lamp out of the corner of my eye, before it smashed into my temple, and I fall towards the bottom of the stairs. I listen to them as I watch blood begin to pool on the floor, impeding my view.

"Oh my Lord. I didn't mean to hit Grace that hard," Stephanie's tone changes. "What should we do?"

"Nothing. If father hears about this, he'll take both our houses away. If we find someone to blame this on, you'll be able to move into this house?" Jessica responds, cunningly.

"Grace never deserved to have this house on the second hill. Father gave her so much more than us. I have an idea, Jessica. Let's blame this on Stan, since Grace says he's not interested in me anyways. We'll keep our houses on the other hills and father will be furious with Stan for killing Grace."

I try to speak and move, but no words form and I can't manage more than a twitch. The pool of blood grows around me.

"Great idea, Stephanie. Father won't suspect we're involved, and we'll gain Grace's house too! Stan will go down for murdering our sister!"

"That's what you get for stealing from me, Grace," Stephanie says, stepping around my body. "Now your boyfriend Stan will pay, too. Yes, we better get out of here before anyone sees us."

I lay on the floor, trying to move to warn Stan of what's happening, but my head' is throbbing. *"Please be safe my love..."*

1988

Mr. Dee came into my office, holding a folder.

"Vincent, go get me some information about the deaths of two those elderly people who died under suspicious circumstances at an old folk's home. Mr. Chadwick, the building's caretaker, has agreed to talk with you," he says.

"Yes, Mr. Dee," I reply, grabbing my notepad, recorder, and the file from Mr. Dee while heading out.

Pulling up to the address, I gasp as I stare at an apartment building standing where the Victorian house stood no more than three years ago. Walking up to the building, a chill runs through me as I remember the evil that occupied this space. Past the front doors, a man approaches me and we shake hands. He introduces himself as Mr. Chadwick and we walk down the hall.

"I honestly don't understand what happened," he starts. "I've never seen two people die like this in any apartment before. They lived right above each other, Roy on the second floor and Mary on the first. He was a kind man, always had a smile on. I don't know how he could die like that."

"How did he die, exactly?" I ask, curiously.

"He was old, not stupid. He would never have tried to stand on his bed like a child. I found him and his head propped up against his bedroom wall. He'd been dead for some time when I found him. The medics say he must have been standing on his bed, but his arthritis was bad. He could never have stood up on his bed even if he wanted to."

"Well, then tell me. What do you think happened?" I ask.

"I don't know. He didn't have any visitors the last couple of days, which is odd. He always had people stopping by, even just to say hi."

"What about the other tenants in the building? Did they see or hear something?"

"There's six tenants here, well…four now. I'm sure they'll tell you what you want to know, but they've said they didn't hear anything."

"How long has this place been here, Mr. Chadwick?"

"They opened the doors three and a half months ago."

"That's a short period of time between opening and these suspicious deaths."

"Yes, too short of time. I hope by telling the story someone finds out what caused it."

"I do, too. What can you tell me about the second person?" I ask.

"Oh, Mary. She lived on the first floor, under Roy's apartment. Her death is even stranger. I found her after I was alerting the other tenants of what happened to Roy. When I got to her room and she didn't answer, I let myself in and found her sitting on the couch. There was a look of fear on her face as if she died of fright. I called for a second ambulance and came back, and noticed she had been in the middle of grabbing her cup of tea. They said she had a heart attack, but I've never seen a heart attack where someone looks like they instantaneously died."

"That's true, usually they're on the floor and their surroundings are disturbed?"

"Exactly! Not sitting up grabbing a cup of tea."

"Did she have any visitors lately?" I ask.

"No. She was looking forward to her grandchildren coming this weekend, but other than that she mainly kept to herself."

"What do you think happened here?" I state.

"I don't know, but I have heard some strange noises. About a month or so ago it sounded like someone heavy was walking around, and there was some scratching on the walls, but when I checked there was nothing there?"

"Ghosts?" I ask.

"I don't believe in ghosts," he scoffs. "I just used that as a reference to how new the place is."

"Can I ask you a question about the building?" I ask, uneasy. "Do you know who built and owns the property?"

"Yes, I have those papers in my office. This way."

We walk right past to the last apartment. He opens the door, and I feel a familiar cold breeze.

"Do you have the air conditioner on?"

"No. It's always cool in these apartments. I get complaints from tenants. Here's the papers I think you're looking for?"

He puts all the papers on his desk. The builder is from out of town, and the owner is also from out of town. I write down their phone numbers and names.

"Thank you for your time."

"You're welcome."

Heading back to my office, I sit down and begin penning the story. Fiddling the pen in my fingers, I come to a stop, deciding to call the builder. I dial the number, and it rings twice before a man answers.

"Hello?"

"Hi! My name is Vincent and I'm calling about an apartment building you built in Saskatoon...?" I start before being cut off.

"God, don't get me started on that place. Yes, we built it, and it cost us a fortune in injuries."

"Injuries?" I ask.

"Yes! That place just did not want to be built. In the seven and a half months we were there, there were 27 injuries. I have worked with these men for a decade and nothing like this has ever happened before. It's the main reason we will never build another house in Saskatoon."

Before I can ask another question, he hangs up on me. Moving on, I call the owner of the apartment.

"Hello?" an older man answers.

"Hi, my name is Vincent. Do you own an apartment building in Saskatoon?" I ask.

"Yes, and I heard about what happened. I am sorry for their loss."

"I was calling to ask who you'd bought the property from."

"I believe I bought it from a church. I paid around $8,000 for the property."

"Did the church mention anything about an evil house that had been there before?" I ask, as thoughts of it drift through my mind.

"They said it used to be a nun's home, but they moved to another location."

"They didn't mention anything about a Victorian house that had been there?"

"Hell, if they had I would've walked away," the man shouts. "Believe me, I should have, but I thought I could trust a church. That building has almost bankrupted me. I'll be almost 70 before I can make a profit and I'm only 48 now."

"Did you call and tell them what happened?"

"Yes They said they'd bless the property, but they never mentioned anything about evil spirits."

"Okay, I'll let you get back to your work. Thanks for your time." I reply, hanging up the phone.

Getting up, I head to St Joseph's church. I walking in and the priest kneeling at the pulpit looks at me. "So why didn't you mention the Victorian house when you sold it?" I ask loudly, approaching him.

"We cleansed the evil from every inch of that property. The house is buried on hallowed ground!"

"You're sure about that? Did you know two people died there yesterday?"

"I'll pray for each of their souls. Perhaps the Lord sent them to be by his side."

"You're a bunch of hypocrites. I found the person you sold that property to and he didn't have a clue about what used to be there. You should have informed him what used to be there but instead you lead him blindly into the mouth of death. Hypocrites. The whole lot of you," I reply, furiously.

"He didn't need to know. We cleaned all the evil out of that property. Whatever happened after that was God's will."

"No, you didn't. That evil is still in there. I felt it when I went to cover the story. It's as strong today as it was when I was last there a few years ago. Face it, you failed against that unknown devil."

"We did our part Vincent," he replies, starting to walk away. "We sent that monster to hell where he belonged. Now please, I must get ready for serv…"

I step in front of him and shout, "it sounds like your church of lies is finally coming to light."

"We didn't lie to anyone. We've always said we cleared the evil out of that house, and we did. What about you, Vincent? Stepping in our way? Trying to pry your nose into our business? What about that?"

"You sure as hell didn't warn anyone. You let them build an apartment over that forsaken land."

"How dare you criticize the church with these blasphemes. Leave now."

"Fine, I'll leave. I'll get to the truth you're trying to hide. Even without those files you stole from my office I'll find what I need to expose this," I answer, infuriated, while walking.

"I don't know of such an event happening, Vincent, but I wish you the best of luck finding them."

I shake my head as I head out of the church. Looking up at the heavens, I wonder, *"He knows where those files are, and doesn't care about the people who have suffered at the hands of that evil. Are they afraid of something more? I guess we'll see where this story leads me."*

Three years earlier

Sitting in the council meeting chamber, I listen as council hears the pleas of various church members.

The mayor calls the meeting to order and starts loudly, "First up, the church has requested to have a Victorian house torn down. We'll hear the complaints."

Person after person states their opinions. Church leaders present evidence of the evil that lives in the house where the three sisters preside. The evidence includes testimony from residents around the house. Accounts of deaths, many failed attempts at boarding it up, and public safety were all questioned.

After the meeting, I stand among the priests, trying to get close enough to hear what Father Daniel McAllister and the other priests had to say about the house and the three sisters. It's in the hands of the city to settle the fate of the house that God damned.

"We believe this house of evil will come down," Father McAllister shouts to the masses. "Whether by God's hands, or by city council. There's no room in this city for the devil, so this house will be no more."

Daniel chatters to other members quietly. Continuing to stand quietly among these members, I listen to them talk about how evil this house is. I take my notepad and my bag, and slip away before anyone notices. Hopping into my car, I drive to the house.

I drive until I see a couple walking down the street and pull over to ask them for directions.

"The three sisters haven't lived there since the late1890's, but just look for the 3 houses on the hill. You can't miss it," they tell me.

Thanking them, I continue on my way, driving until I come to an ominous hill that looks like it leads right to the river. I stop when I get to the second hill, and am shocked by what I see. The house is a dull black Victorian building that is boarded up. Getting out, I head towards the building. As I step on the grass, an old man from across the street yells at me.

"What the hell do you think you're doing? Get away from there!"

I start walking over to ask why, but before I can get close enough, he backs off and starts walking back into his house.

"Excuse me, sir. Why don't you want me going into the yard?" I ask politely.

"That house is pure evil son."

"What do you mean evil?" I answer.

Looking at him, he seems to be in his early 70's. His hair is gray and his face wrinkled, and he's wearing a priest's collar.

"Are you a priest?" I ask.

"I used to be, but I'm retired now."

"You must know something about that house. Who owns it?"

"That house is evil. The devil resides within those walls, waiting to take innocent souls."

"What can you tell me about the owners of the house?" I try again.

"They've all passed on. All that's left is the devil and the lost souls of his victims."

"Who owns the house now?"

"The devil. I see him watching me, waiting, to take more souls with him to Hell."

"The devil can't possibly own it."

"He does, and if you step foot on that property, I'll pray for your soul. If I were you, I'd walk away."

He closes the door before I can ask him anything further. Turning to look at the house, there's no real damage to it other than the boarded-up windows. It almost looks livable. Crossing the street, I look back at the ld man's house and see the curtain shimmy a bit.

Getting to the yard once again, I looking at the house and wal around to the back. At the back porch, the door is slightly ajar. Creeping up, I open the door just a little bit and a stale odor wafts out. I hear noises coming from inside, but they're soft. Little bangs and creaking stairs. I debate within myself if I should continue or not.

My shadow is devoured by the darkness. Looking further inside, it looks like a shiny coin is sitting in the middle of the kitchen. The longer I stand watching, the more enticing it become.

Closing the door, I walk away. I can hear the creaking as I walk to the front yard again. I decide to ask others in the neighborhood about the house. I walk next door, but nobody answers. I leave my business card and move on. This continues for the rest of the day until I head back to my car and leave.

I decide to head to the library to see if I can find anything in the archives about the house. I spend a few hours looking, but only come up with a few possibilities. I quit searching for the night.

As I'm packing up, the phone rings.

"Hello?"

The caller is one of the people I left a card for. They want to meet me, but away from the area, so we agree to meet a while later at the McDonald's. I gather everything I need- a tape recorder, pens, and paper- and head over. When I arrive, there are a few people inside. I walk around until I come to a husband and wife in their mid-sixties, looking at me closely.

"Are you Brian?" I ask.

"Yes, please have a seat."

Sitting down, I pull out my paper and pen.

"On the phone, you said you had something to tell me?" I begin.

"Yes, I do. We saw you yesterday walking around the house. The church forbids anyone from going there. You've already met one of their people. He tries to get people away from there. The last people who lived there were a young couple who had 2 children."

"What're their names?" I ask, getting ready to write it down.

"I don't rightly know their names. Besides, I wouldn't want anything to leave this conversation."

"I don't understand. Why's everyone so secretive about this house?" I ask.

"Around 1964, this family moved in. There were 3 of them. Everything was fine for the first couple years. They have another child, a little girl named Sandy. She was cute as a button. One day, their dad came home and found his wife dead, at the bottom of the stairs. They said she died of a sharp knife, but just her and her kids were there. Harry, their son, had said the devil did it. He said his mom was coming upstairs and the devil was following her. He said the devil picked her up and slammed her against the wall by the stairs. That poor boy just kept saying the devil did it. They put him in an asylum."

"An asylum in town?" I reply.

"Yes. They thought he must have suffered a great shock by his mother's death."

"That's too bad. Is he still there?"

"I'm not sure. We haven't kept in contact since they left."

"Is there anything you can remember that'll help me?" I continue.

"That place has been plagued by death since about the early 1900s. You know why they call it the three sister's right?"

"Because it's owned by three sisters?" I guess.

"That's what we heard, too. Around 1885, there were 3 plots of land bought with a house on each hill. For the first while, everything was great between the sisters, but then a man came courting the sister that lived in the house on the second hill. The other sisters' jealousy was overwhelming. It seems they got together and schemed to get their sister out of the way. One stormy night, they came in and killed her. Left her bleeding in the living room. A few days later, her man came and found her dead. He packed up and left town. One of the sisters came to check on her and found her right where they left her. They blamed the guy and buried her in the cemetery. They cleaned up what they could of the blood, but you could always see the discolored parts by the stairs.

Seven months later, under a year after her death, one of the sisters slipped walking up the stairs and broke her neck on the way down. A year after, the other sister was washing the floors. She went to stand up, slipped, and broke her neck on the side table. After there was no one left to look after the houses, they sold them to other people. There are no problems with the other two houses, just that one. A family moved in in 1901, and within 6 months the father fell down those stairs and died. His wife and their children had to move out because they couldn't afford to live there. The house sold again in 1903, this time to a man ready for a family. He was fixing up the house until one day he just quit coming out of the house. He became a recluse and in about June of 1904 they found him hanging from the banister of the stairs."

"That's far too many deaths for one house," I exclaim.

"It gets worse, Vincent. After they found him, they went to the basement and found the sign of the devil- a pentagram."

"A real pentagram?" I ask.

"Yes, carved into the dirt floor. They sold it again, but this time to a minister and his wife. They were told about the previous owners but still bought it. In 1905, they were arguing and one ended killing the other one."

"I can't believe that all happened in one house," I state, shaking my head thinking this guy is nuts.

"Don't mock it. That house is evil. There are times where my wife and I wake to the screams that come from that house!"

Looking over at his wife, she nods her head.

"I'm sorry, I meant no disrespect. What happened next?" I try to keep the conversation going.

"It sold again in 1907. This time to an Irish couple and their children. They moved out just 3 months after they moved in. Their children were talking to someone in the basement and it scared the hell out of him so they packed up and left. I can't tell you anymore, but I know someone who lived near there. I don't know if he remembers anything though."

"It could only help me," I answer.

"The last morsel of information I can tell you is that that house has been through many people's hands. Most have not lived to tell the tales of what happened there."

"You've got my number if you contact that person?"

"I do, and I will call tomorrow."

"Thank you for sitting and talking with me." I state, standing and heading for the door.

I sit at home trying to process what I had learned. *"Was what they told me…was it true? That many people dying at one house over that short period of time? There must be information about that house floating around somewhere?"*

That night is full of nightmares about people dying with the devil standing there, laughing at me, the whole time.

The phone rings, waking me, and I look over at the clock. 7:02 a.m. I grab the phone and answer.

After a groggy question, I hang up with a new meeting to talk about the house with another man.

Getting up and out the door, I drive to Homestyle Brew. Walking in and looking around, I see an old guy sitting in the corner. He looks to be in his eighties. He has gray hair and a plaid shirt on. Walking over to him, I sit down and just as I'm about to greet him, he leans over and grabs my wrist.

"Listen to me, you stupid prick," he whispers, menacingly. "Did you even consider what you are doing? That house you want to know about is evil. You are here trying to get information and that house hears what you say. Do you understand? It hears everything you say. Every time you breathe it knows. My wife died walking our dog last week. She died in front of that house. The paramedics got there, and that damned house started pulling her towards it. The paramedic told me it took six people to get my wife off the grass. She weighs less than a hundred pounds but it took six people to pick her up off the ground. The dog's leash was still in my wife's hands, so you tell me what happened to it."

"I don't know what could've happened to your dog?" I reply, confused.

"I do. That house wants and needs more souls to feed on. I bet you a dollar if I go there, I'll find my dog and then I'll die when I go to get him. That's how that house gets you. It dangles whatever you love the most and as soon as you move to get it, BAM! You're dead!"

"Come on, you can't honestly believe that!" I reply.

"You want proof. Let's go there right now and I'll prove it to you."

"Only if you're sure you want to."

"I am damn sure! Let's go!"

The employees stare as we head out to my car. We drive to the house and pull over. He walks towards the house and stops. Coming up beside him, I stand there, watching.

"Get away from that damned house!" the man across the street yells from his doorstep.

"No, father, I have to prove this house is evil. I have already lost my wife," the man with me yells back.

He starts walking again into the yard, and points to the grass. "You see that on the grass? That's where my wife died."

Looking towards the ground, I see a slight imprint in the grass. We go around to the back of the house, and the elderly man stops by the door. I look at him closely and see the fear in his eyes.

"Goddam you! You killed my wife and took my dog," he yells, shaking.

I stand on the porch looking at him, and start to get the feeling that someone is watching us, but I shake it off as paranoia. He grabs the door and flings it open, still yelling. Before I can say anything, the door flies back and hits him into the house. He screams as I open the door and pull him out.

"Are you okay?" I ask.

"I'm fine. Did you see that?"

"I did. The door come back and hit you."

"No. That house threw me into it. I saw something coming towards me, holding its evil hands out to grab me, just before you pulled me out."

"The house tried to throw you into it? I'm going to have to go, but I'll drop you off at your car," I reply, rolling my eyes.

"Yes, yes it did! You saw that with your own eyes. You'll stop with all this nonsense now?"

"Okay, I'll quit looking into it," I reply, humoring him

I drive to work and there are three calls waiting for me. The secretary lets me know there's someone in my office waiting for me as well. Walking in, there is a woman in her seventies sitting waiting.

"A friend of mine told me you were looking for information about that old Victorian place," she says, looking up at me.

"Yes, I am. I have heard some strange stories about it so far," I say, sitting down.

"Oh dear, yes. And they're all true too!"

"They can't all be real," I state.

"We'll see about that after I tell you what I know."

"Okay," I respond, pulling out my tape recorder.

"In 1956, my now deceased husband and I moved there on April 1st. We were happy as could be. My husband, George, had been making the basement a full basement. After a couple of months, I noticed George becoming more and more irritated. I asked him one night what was going on and he told me there was something in the basement saying it would torture me if George didn't finish the basement in 3 months. I guess it must've been true. Another night, George wasn't feeling well so he didn't go into the basement at all that day. I broke my leg walking down the stairs. It was like someone picked me up and broke my leg before I even hit the floor."

She shakes her head, sniffles, and continues.

"When we got home from the Doctor, he grabbed his tools and he spent the rest of the evening in the basement. I heard him saying "sorry, don't hurt my wife again," over and over again. I could sense something down there with him, and there was an almost arctic cold breeze coming from the basement. Once he finished, we moved out. I didn't understand until George told me that it took him 3 more days to finish it and that he'd been warned that any longer would result in death. George died a month after we moved."

"I see. Did anything else happen while you were there?" I ask.

"You know, come to think of it, yes. I thought I saw a black figure shortly after we moved in. It looked evil, like it wanted to come after me, but I was wearing my mother's cross necklace so I don't think it could have."

"Yes, I can imagine."

"I hope this helps you find what you are looking for."

"Every little bit helps. Thank you again for coming in." I reply. "You're welcome. I'll leave my number with the woman out front."

"Okay, thank you." I reply, sitting back. I wonder if everyone who lived in or around that house is crazy. I check the three messages on my machine. The first just says to leave the house alone and the second warns me of danger. The third message is from someone who says they can help me if we meet at the house tonight. I sit there, rereading the messages, wondering if it will be another crazy whack job? I remember what that one guy told me about Harry and scramble to find the name and head for the asylum.

When I get to the asylum, the woman at the front greets me and asks who I am there to see.

"I'm looking for Harry. He would've come here 67-68 sometime in 1967 or 1968."

"Oh, yes. Harry Henderson. A tragic case. He saw his mother killed," the woman immediately replies.

"Yes, he might have some information I need?" I continue.

"Oh, are you working on finding the killer?"

"Yes and no. I know he heard someone talking to his mother."

"Yes, he refers to him as the devil!"

"That sounds like him," I answer.

"Follow me then. He's on the first floor."

We walk, and I listen to the moans of the patients. We finally come to a room at the end of the hall.

"Harry? You have a visitor," she says softly, opening the door.

Looking inside, I see Harry is in a straitjacket, sitting in the corner.

"Try not to upset him, okay?" the nurse says, turning to me.

"I'll do my best no to." I answer as she closes the door behind me. I sit down on the floor across from Harry and pull the tape recorder out.

"What's that?" he asks.

"It records what we say," I reply.

"I've never seen one of those before."

"I bet. Can I ask you some questions?" I ask quietly.

"Sure, what do you want to know?"

"Well, I am looking into what happened at your house many years ago," I start.

"Oh, you want to know about the devil."

"Yes, I want you to tell me everything you can from beginning to end."

"Okay, but I don't think you'll believe me. Nobody else has."

"Trust me, I have heard some strange stories this week. Yours can't be any worse." I reply, as he gives me a strange look.

"Well, I can remember that my sister and I used to play in the basement a lot. We would see this little boy sitting in the corner. He was almost cowering. He'd say weird stuff like "quit looking at me" or "oh no, he's coming". We couldn't see anything, but that boy was scared. I think it was a couple of days later that my sister Sandy was downstairs talking to someone. She kept saying she wasn't going to do something, then she screamed and had a red mark on her face. I ran to her, but I felt two hands push me and I flew across the room. I saw the face of something dark. It had red eyes and when it grabbed me and picked me up it said I would die in that house. I belonged to him and so did everyone else who set foot in those four walls.

I could see the hate in his eyes, almost as if he was human. I didn't want to be there any longer. He threw me down and went for my sister. He picked her up and told me he would have a special place for her if we didn't do as he said. We told him yes and then he went after the boy in the corner who was standing up. My mom heard his screams because she came running downstairs. She looked at us, saw Sandy's red face, and blamed me. There was another time when he came with a woman. Her dress looked old and it was much too big on her..."

"You mean a Victorian dress?" I ask.

"Yes," he nods. "I guess something like that. He said this was the one who brought him to the house, and she is paying for every minute he's cursed to this house. He reached into her chest and pulled out her heart, then shoved it back in. She begged him to stop, crying, and he threw her into the wall where she vanished. He grabbed me next squeezed my ribs. He told I'd be the next one to see a loved one go through pure pain for eternity. He let go and disappeared again. I was fearing for my life by that time, and I didn't know what to think or do."

He stops and tries scratching his nose before continuing.

"A week before it killed mom, Sandy and I had gone down to the basement. He hadn't been there for a few weeks so we figured it would be okay but boy were we wrong. We got down there, and he was standing with hundreds of people crushed in the corner. He said all the people belonged to him. He said he had warned us and now someone had to pay. He grabbed Sandy and threw her at the people. Her screams for help fell silent as they covered her mouth. He hovered towards me, picked me up by the shirt, and said I had a choice. He asked me to pick between my sister and my mother. I didn't know what to do. I said mom so he would let Sandy go. I didn't think he could hurt her. He haunted my dreams, showing me what would happen to mom, and I couldn't fall asleep. I just cried for hours and hours."

"The day before she died, I told her about what happened and that she was going to die. She told me to quit reading so many comics. I told her the truth, but she didn't believe me. The next day she took a box downstairs. She was down there for a while before she came back up, and he was following her. I tried to tell mom to look out, but I think he knew that because he lifted her up by her neck. She could finally see him. He screamed at her and banged her against the wall. I think mom died before she hit the floor. She just went limp. He pulled her out of her body. She was screaming for him to let her go. He let her go, and she ran to hug me, but he just laughed. He said she was there to stay."

He stopped again as banged his head against the padded wall, clearly upset.

"Mom ran for the door but stopped short. He yelled, "You belong to me!" I couldn't understand why mom didn't keep running. I didn't see anything there and the door was open, but he was still laughing. He told me my sister was going to be next. I was still sitting there, watching, when dad walked in and saw mom laying there. He ran over asking what had happened. I told him the devil did it, but dad couldn't seem to see it. I just kept saying what I saw and they eventually took me here. To this day, nobody believes me."

"I believe you. My god! What happened to your sister and dad?"

"I don't know. They have never been here to visit me," he replies, tears rolling down his face.

"I'll see if I can track them down for you," I reply.

"I would like to see my sister again."

"I'll see what I can do then. No promises though."

"I know. I would just like to know they're okay."

"Thanks for talking with me, Harry," I say, standing up.

"Thank you for listening. I feel better knowing someone believes me."

I open the door and walk out. Getting to my car, I start feeling what it must have been like for a child in that house. I think about the meeting tonight and an uneasy chill creeps up my spine.

Waiting until close to 11 PM, I drive over to the house. I walk to the backyard and a dark figure is standing by the door.

"You want to know about me, do you?" a dark voice echoes.

"If you want to tell me."

"Great, come on in?"

"No thank you. Out here is just fine," I state as he laughs.

"I see someone is believing the tales he has heard?"

"Yes, I do. What do you have to tell me?" I ask.

"Well, that depends on what you believe."

"I believe there is evil here."

"You're damn right there is."

"What is the name of the evil living in the house?"

"Are you a priest or reporter, Vincent?"

"A reporter."

"Then I guess you'd better report."

"What's your name?" I ask. "Jesus?"

"Watch your tongue, little man," he growls. "You never know when that tongue is going to be your undoing."

"Then what's your name?" I ask again.

"I have no name. I was here long before any person walked on this planet."

"Well, if you have no name, where are you from?" I respond. Cautiously.

"Earth, you fucking moron!"

"…Sorry, I thought you might be from someplace else?" I state, taken aback.

"Just because a book says God was here first doesn't mean anything. Do you want the real truth or do you want the truth according to a book? People who rely on others to provide them with a truth are weak. The truth hangs in your personal beliefs that belong to you. If you need a book to tell you how to be good, then how can you be sure of its truth? The truth is a balance of everything, including lies. Vincent, you report news, but what truths do you conceal in amongst a twist of words? Now, what would you like to hear?"

"The truth. I want the real truth!" I state.

"Good. I'll tell you, but on one condition."

"What's that?" I ask.

"You must take these items with you and place them in the city here," he says, stretching out his hand, holding several small talismans. "Deal?"

"That's the only condition?" I ask.

"Yes. These five items must be safe, or I'll come for you and everyone you love."

"I'll make sure nothing happens to them," I reply, as he hands them over.

I look at what he's given me and it looks like garbage. A piece of wood, a piece carpet, a couple of pence, and a rock.

"Just make sure they aren't destroyed."

"I promise." I state, watching him closely.

"Okay, Vincent, the truth. The head of the house died many years ago and it was a bloody mess. Her blood seeped into the ground. She died at the perfect time and I was summoned to the house. However, this woman's blood, and the way she died, turned me into a spirit again. Now, I am attached to this house forever."

"What about Harry's sister?" I ask.

"Well, I guess you want to jump ahead? Okay, his sister is doing fine. Would you like to ask her yourself?"

"Beg your pardon? You mean you have her?" I answer, shocked.

"Yes, I have everyone who has ever lived here."

"Can I talk to her?" I ask.

"Is it going to ease your soul if you do?"

"It would."

I hear a scream and a silhouette comes to the door. An apparition of a little girl stands in the doorway.

"Tell Harry I'm sorry," she says, her voice almost inaudible.

"I will," I reply, as she disappears again.

"There, you spoke to her. Is your soul happier? Is there anything else you'd like before I continue, Vincent?"

"There was so much I wanted to ask her."

"I let you talk to her. I didn't say you could have a long talk with her."

"Okay, I get it. I'm just saying I would've liked to. Go on with what you were saying!"

"Every person who's lived or died here belongs here. I make sure everyone comes back. I even have a dollhouse of this place that's gone to many homes. They are mine too! You think believing in a God saves you from bad things happening, but it doesn't. I'll let you in on a secret. I have a total of 31 priests in here, and they thought they could get rid of me too. They lay there holding their precious charms for protection. They may have boarded up the windows, but they just couldn't finish the job. Their God hasn't taken them home yet, nor will he. They belong here, and here's where they'll stay!"

"What's this about a dollhouse?" I ask curiously.

"It's a replica of this house. Anyone who brings it home with them can see what's in the house, but it makes them curious," he smiles in the dark.

"I have to ask, why me?"

"I saw you yesterday. You wanted so bad to come in, but you hesitated. I thought you would be a good one to tell these victim's stories. After all, isn't that what you do?"

"Yes, but I tell the truth in my stories," I answer.

"Exactly! That's why you must tell other people about this house. The poor victims who have suffered so much pain. You see, I too believe that everyone can do some good, but you are only as good as what you do for others. They want you to believe God helps you when you're good. He doesn't. When people do evil, it's blamed on the devil, but it is only you that has the power to do good or bad."

"I'll let people know, but I have to ask. If there's no devil and no God, then what are you?"

"I told you, I was here long before anyone ever stood on this ground. I am not evil, even though I said I was. I am me. I don't claim to be good or bad, others do that for me. I am letting you know these portions for a reason. You must keep their spirits alive. Those items I gave you, they are soon to be the only remains of the house. Those five items are the only memory for these people who died inside the house. You destroy those valuables, and you destroy their essence. The hour nears. Remember what I said…"

Before I can respond, a wind blows and the door slams shut. *"Was that real?"* I think to myself, as look at my hand and see I'm holding those items. Walking quickly around the house, I hear screams of pain and wonder what would happen if I didn't do as he said. No, I had better do it. I don't want anyone else to die. I go home and go to bed.

The next day, I get another call saying a man wants to talk, so I agree and I head out to meet him. I walk around Kinsmen Park, looking for someone wearing a red hat, until finally I see them sitting on the rocks, under the pass. I walk over and sit down.

"So, you're the one. A little young to be treading these waters, aren't you?" he glares at me.

"Yes, I'm Vincent. The one that's what?" I ask, confused.

"You're the one ticking people off."

"I guess so."

"You've seen it, haven't you?"

"Last night, how can you tell?" I reply, shocked.

"You have a coldness about you. What did it say or do?"

"Whatever that was told me that it's killed priests and tons of people there."

"Yes, I was one of the priests there that fateful day trying to board up the house so no one else would die in there."

"Can you tell me more?" I ask.

"I'll tell you only because I am dying, so there is nothing the church can do to me! It was July 17th, 1978. I was only one of 20 priests sent in. We were told God had our backs and no matter what, we shouldn't show fear. I went upstairs with 14 others caring plywood to cover the windows. It smelled rotten, like death. We were throwing holy water in all directions. We divided into groups to cover more space and each of the rooms faster. We were putting the first set of blessed nails into the plywood covering the windows, when darkness hit and out of nowhere came this dark figure, slamming Father O'shay right into one of the nails sticking out, impaling him. Father Danker was next."

"I ran for my life! Every room was darkened and everyone was screaming bloody murder. He slammed me into the wall and told me I was making a big mistake. I told him I was doing God's work. He told me God only exists because humans can't cope with anything that we do. He gave me a chance to get out of his house and I did just that. I ran down the stairs, stumbling on my colleague that had fallen by these demons, mauled to death. I finally got to the main floor and the blood was pouring down the stairs like a waterfall. I start running once again and Father O'keefe was hanging by the back door! I make a straight line for the door, only to find another whose face was ripped off. He was pulled back to the basement stairs right before my eyes."

He stops and takes a few breathes before continuing.

"I was just about outside when Father Neil's body hit the back window, smashing glass all over the place. I still have the scars from the glass that nearly slit my throat. Just as I was going out the door, something pulled me into the living room. All I could feel was the burning. It felt like a thousand cats scratching me at the same time. I plead for God to save me, then that dark one was standing in front of me again. He told me he would do something God couldn't. He gave me four seconds to get out of the house. You'd better believe I ran out of that house. Father James came in to close the door and board it up from the inside. I pushed him out of the way to get out of that door. Outside, Father Sam asked what happened. I told him Father James had been grabbed and thrown off to the side. That lie still haunts me to this day. You must understand, I wanted to live."

"I do understand. Can you at least give your name?" I ask.

"Francis. The priests died in that house, Vincent. Seventeen of them. The light of the cross from the church shining brightly on the house did nothing to stop the killing."

"What happened after you left, Father?"

"Well, Father Johnson and Father Smith bandaged my neck up to stop the bleeding. The screams kept coming from the house, crying out to God to help them. Father Smith went running for the door, and the other two with him doused the door with holy water before they sent in three more to try to board the door up from the inside."

"What happened to them?"

"They started off fine, but then the door was flung wide open! Father Jenzen's face exploded right before my eyes as if someone punched him in his head. I still can't believe what I saw. He was dragged back into the house and I don't know what happened next. Those poor souls screamed in agony until they fell silent."

"Did the rest of you manage to get out?" I ask.

"You'd think they would have, but the church was unwavering. They were determined to seal that place up. They thought they could close it up before anything happened to anyone else. It was a blood bath. Not one of us left that house unsoiled by the end. We ended with the windows and front door boarded up, but we just couldn't get that back door. 21 were dead and left to rot in that house. No burials, just dead"

"I am so sorry about that. Did no one try to go back to get them?"

"Here and there they did, but I doubt anyone even went close to the house. They would make their excuses, but they were scared. Everyone was told not to mention the house. The church believed in that creature more than God."

"You mean those priests are still there?" I ask, shocked.

"Oh yes. They are forever in there until that evil leaves," he nods.

"You mentioned not being allowed to talk about it. Why?"

"The church screwed up. They sent people thinking God was with them in their dictation to enter that house. God was not there, and it was just us against him and he won. The church does what they do best when they make a mistake, they cover it up. They told people that they were on a mission of God in another province or another country, and they died helping others, when in reality they are lying dead in that house. We protested, but our pleas were never replied to. There are four of us left who were there. We made a pact that if one of us died we would tell someone what happened, so these families may get the closure they need to move on. So, here I am."

"Thank you for talking to me."

"You're welcome, but I still have more to say."

"Please, continue."

"They have the house's history locked away in vaults. No one can find out about that house. They've hidden everything about that house, making sure there's nothing left to find. The only piece left to deal with is tearing the house down, and once that happens there will be no records of it ever existing."

"So that's why I can't find anything out," I say, finally understanding.

"Once the church finds out that someone talked, they'll threaten everyone else who knows. It's a mafia of sorts, strong-arming people to be quiet."

"They can't do that, can they?" I answer, shocked.

"The church feels they can do whatever it takes to make people see their way. This house is no different. They will do what they have to to make sure no one knows what happened there. There's a priest that lives across from the house and he tells the church whenever people stop by."

"Is he part of the church, or does he just live there?"

"He's part of the church. They send retired and active priests there to watch and make sure no one enters the house. That house hasn't had people living in it since 1972. I don't know how far they have gone to keep people away from there. Knowing the church, they'd take it as far as they had to."

"I talked with that boy, Harry. He told me what happened."

"Harry? Yes, of course. His family was the last to live there. A sad story. He told everyone what he saw, and the church saw to it that he was confined to the asylum. I feel for him and hope he is doing okay."

"He was happy that I believed him."

"Yes, I bet he was. Nobody would listen to him. Had they listened we might not have lost so many good souls that day."

"Can I ask you something personal?" I ask, changing the topic.

"I'll answer as best I can."

"That thing told me that anyone who lived there, or came there, belonged to the house. I wonder how you could get out with your life?"

"I wish I knew. Twice he let me go, and I have no idea why. I should be laying upstairs, a bloody corpse, with my colleagues. There are days I wish I were dead, and others where I am thankful to be alive. I think he is God in disguise. He could have killed me as easy as any of the others, but he chose to let me go."

"He also mentioned a dollhouse," I continue.

"Yes, I heard this from others and I believe it to be true. There was a girl, Candice I believe her name was …beautiful girl who found this dollhouse in an alley near her house. She brought it home and started playing with it. Her parents let her keep it. Well, I guess the house started playing the part, as this little girl would see ghosts in the dollhouse. After a few days or a little longer, she saw the real house and decided to go in. Sadly, she was never seen again. I can't guarantee this, but I have heard it from people who were close."

"Oh, dear, that sounds bad. This dollhouse is a magnet of evil?"

"Yes, I would say this dollhouse's sole purpose is to bring people to the house."

"Do you know where I might find that girl's parents?" I ask.

"I wouldn't expect them to cooperate."

"Because of the church's influence?" I ask, confused.

"No, they're having a hard time believing that a dollhouse took their daughter."

"Do you know of anyone else who has seen the dollhouse?"

"I do, but I can't promise they'll talk to you. I can call you later if they are willing."

"That's great. You have my number?"

"Yes, I do."

"Is there anything else you would like to tell me?"

"Yes, be careful. You're opening several old wounds. Wounds these people want to go away."

"Thanks, I'll take care of anything that comes my way."

"Can you hold off for at least a month before writing this story? I'd be grateful. I should be dead within the month according to what the doctors tell me."

"Yes, I can do that, considering all the information you have given me."

"Thank you. Go in peace, my son."

I sit here and watch as he slowly makes his way to the path, never turning around, and disappears into the distance. Pondering what he has told me, I head for my office, sit at my desk, and start writing down some of the information. Mary walks in, and hands me more messages. I read through a few before I get to one that reads, "Please contact me about the dollhouse!" Could it be that he got ahold of them that fast? I call the number, and a woman picks up. She tells me she has seen the dollhouse and to meet her somewhere on the west side of the city. We make plans to meet outside Confederation mall. Getting there early, I grab myself something to eat. When I get back, there is a woman in her twenties standing outside, looking around. I walk up to her and ask, "are you waiting for someone?"

"Yes, I'm waiting for you," she replies, looking at my notepad.

We head over to a quiet spot in the parking lot and sit down. "You said on the phone you had something to tell me about a dollhouse?"

"Yes, I do. My daughter had brought this dollhouse home with her, and she said she found it on the street. I let her keep it because it looked clean enough. A few days go by and she starts telling me about some horrific images in the dollhouse, so I go check but I can't see anything. The next day my daughter, Amanda, says there's something else in the dollhouse. Again, I go look and see nothing. Yesterday a friend of mine told me there was a guy leaving cards, looking into a house, so I figured you may know something about this."

"Well, I'm learning a lot about the house connected to this dollhouse. Please continue to tell me about what was happening?" I answer.

"Well, like I said, there was nothing there before yesterday ..."

"Wait, you're telling me you just got it this week?" I answer, shocked.

"Yes, do you want to see it?"

I stand up, dumbfounded. *"Is she for real? Is she going to show me this dollhouse?"*

"Umm. Yes, please."

We walk to her van and she opens the doors to reveal an exact replica of the house. My breath leaves momentarily as I gaze at the dollhouse.

"As I was saying, yesterday Amanda said there was something in the dollhouse again. I went to look and this time I could see someone hanging by the door. I freaked out and it sounded like someone was speaking, but it was quiet. I couldn't understand what they were saying."

I kneel down to get a better look. I see at least seven dead bodies lying in the living room. There's a man hanging by the door, swaying back and forth. I look on the stairs going up, and two more images of people are lying there as if they had falling down. Inspecting the whole house, it's full of similar scenes. I fall back, feeling an eerie sense, and throw up.

"Are you okay, Vincent?" she asks, concerned.

"Yes, it must've been something I ate this morning," I say, trying to smile.

"So, can you help us?"

"I think I can. If you want to give it to me, I'll take it to someone who may know what's going on. Here's a card for you, it has my home number on it, just in case something happens," I reply.

"Okay, this is your problem now. I have to go see my daughter in the hospital."

"What happened?" I ask.

"She reached into the dollhouse and something scratched her. This morning it was red and patchy."

"Well, I hope she feels better."

"I know I will, knowing that isn't in my house anymore."

"I can believe it," I whisper to myself, carrying the dollhouse with me to my car. I put it in the backseat and drive home. Putting it on my table at home, I go back to work.

In the evening, I make some coffee and over at the dollhouse. Sitting down to look at it closely, a dark figure forms at the bottom of the stairs and looks at me.

"Why do you have the dollhouse?" a voice asks, barely audible.

"I met with a woman whose daughter picked it up," I state.

"You do realize why the house goes to certain people, right," it asks, angry.

"If I remember right, you said it brings people to you?"

"Yes, it brings people to me. You have the dollhouse which means that girl isn't coming to the house."

"I'm sorry, I didn't realize."

"Fine, I'll move the dollhouse tomorrow. Touch it again and you'll be here next."

"I have to ask you something."

"You're beginning to irritate me, Vincent. What do you want?"

"How did you show yourself to me the other night for that long?"

"I told you I've been around longer than anything on this planet. I talked to you on the phone, too. I can do a great many deeds. The priests believe the witching hour is 3 AM, but it starts at 11 PM. That's when my power is greatest. Anything else?"

"What I saw in the dollhouse… were those the priests?"

"Yes, they were. To this day, they stay where I want them too. No one moves if they know what's good for them."

"I was talking with father…?" start.

"Yes, I know," he interrupts. "And you want to know why I let him go, right?"

"Yes, I would?"

"I'll tell you, but it's going to cost you."

"Cost me what?" I ask, curiously.

"I see that you haven't put those items anywhere yet. I want you to keep one of those items for yourself."

"Okay, I swear I will keep one."

"I let him live because I saw the fear in his face. When I grabbed him and threw him, his fear of dying was my rush. He was Godless when he came up those stairs. When he saw the first priest impaled, he knew he was close to death. I gave him a choice and he chose life."

His laugh sends shivers throughout me, as he continues, "I let him live so he could tell others to stay away."

"I see. What about these girls? I know one came to the house after the dollhouse?"

"Do you ever get sick of questions?"

"Questions get you answers," I state.

"She came for the prize but got a surprise instead. Look at the couch, see her sitting there?"

"Yes, I can see her, but why is she just sitting there?" I ask, puzzled.

"She's dead. The house was hungry and needed someone pure."

"Why though? Why not an elderly person. Someone who's lived a full life?"

"Old people don't play with dollhouses, little girls and boys do."

"Why don't you use something else that doesn't attract children?"

"You mean like a gold watch or ring? How would those trinkets bring people to the house? They wouldn't. I need something that will bring them here. Once here the house decides what it wants from them. I provide the outlet."

"That's a little harsh? I mean they are only kids?" I state, as he replies,

"Yes, the world's cruel and we're all living for survival. I didn't ask to be here, but here I am. I do what I have to do to survive. You need food, right?"

"Yes, bu…?"

"You'd die if you didn't eat. If you had to kill for a bite, no matter how big or small, would you do it? Just to live one more day? I do the same to survive."

"Yes, I can see that, but there have to be better ways."

"Not all children die. When they come, there's a few that see the beauty of the house. They don't die, they just enjoy the time spent here. I don't go and lure them in, they come and go as far as they wish to."

Pankratz

"Are there children inside I can talk with?" I ask.

"No. Not unless you come when they are here. They don't come every day, and they don't come regularly. They come when they want the company of the house. When they are hurting and need a shoulder that isn't there for them."

"So, it's okay for some children coming here, but not all children? I don't understand?"

"Listen, I am going to tell you a story of people. Your people, and the people of the world. Thousands of years ago, when the people were new, they figured out that the strongest survived. They'd hold fights, feats of strength, proving they had what it takes to be a leader. At the first sign of weakness, they'd kill that one and replace them with someone more capable. This is still a monumental event to this day. As the years passed by, they grew tired of the same thing happening. Therefore, they would travel many miles to find new ways to get more power. They would raid other villages, and they always killed the children of their enemies so they couldn't rise to crush them one day. Then the day came that religion was created.

Whether you talk Gods, or God, the result is the same. You follow or you die. They found a thief who was crucified for his punishment, and they made a martyr out of his stinking remains. They moved him out of the chamber where he was laid and created the miracle of life from death. Everyone's wanting in on the action, and begins believing the hype. So now, you have thousands of people trying to create new religions that'll have everyone entranced to the beauty of what is in them. You can call me a monster, or whatever you like, but I am not the one who created a way to massacre the masses of children. The house has taken seventeen children over many years here, which in no way compares with the hundreds of millions of children taken in the name of religion."

"I didn't know."

"Of course you wouldn't know. You have lived but 28 years. Believe it or not, it happened and is happening as we speak. I said it enough times, I didn't want to be here. I do what I have to do to survive. Is there anything else you want to know before I move this dollhouse?"

"Nothing comes to mind right now?"

"Finally! I thought you'd never shut up? Go to bed and when you wake the dollhouse will be gone. And yes, before you ask, this is real. Remember our deal."

I watch him walk up the tiny stairs and vanish with all the victims.

Getting up in the morning, I look towards the table shocked. "The dollhouse is gone!" I shout. Looking around, can't find it, and suddenly remember what happened. I getting ready for the day and head to city hall.

Walking into the chambers at 8:30 AM, Reverend Danial McAllister is standing at the podium listening to a city councilor.

"Alright, you want us to believe that everything you handed us previously is real?" the councilor asks.

"Yes, sir," Daniel replies.

"Why then have you brought us the land deed to the house that says the land has belonged to the family of Isabella Deonta?"

"That's wrong!" father McAllister answers.

"I don't know about that," another councilor says, standing up. "We are checking to see if we can find her remaining family members. If we can, we will return the deed to them and the land will be there's again. If we can't, we will then consider your recommendation to demolish the house."

"I think you'll find out quickly there is no family left in the city, or anywhere else," the father responds. "Isabella was the last of her family and after her passing, she had no children to pass it on to."

"We will take it under advisement," a woman responds.

"This meeting is closed until we reached our final decision," the mayor shouts.

Walking out, I hear the Reverend talking to another man about a girl who's been around the house for a couple of years. They want to make sure she won't say anything to anyone. I watch the crowd disperse and see a girl heading towards the house. I follow as she walks onto the block then stops. The old man comes out screaming, and runs after her. She looks at him and starts walking towards the house again, the priest following.

After a long engagement of words, he finally retreats to his house. She sits there, and I can see her mouth move as if she is talking to someone. After watching her for a couple of hours, she looks straight at me. She laughs and motions for me to come over, so I make my way over with my recorder. As I walk onto the property, the priest makes his way outside again.

"I'll pray for your burning soul!" he yells.

"You'll be burning first!" the girl shouts back.

"Sit?" she asks, looking up at me, smiling.

"Why did you follow me?" she asks as I sit down.

"I overheard some people talking about a girl who came to this house, and I wanted to meet that girl."

"What do you want?"

"Well, I was wondering if I could ask you a few questions."

"It's a free country, ask whatever you want."

"Thank you. What about that guy that tried to chase you away from here?" I ask.

"That old fart?" she laughs. "He always chases me, but he's all talk and no action."

"Why does he chase you?"

"He doesn't like anyone talking to the people in the house. I only come and sit by the house before going back home."

"Does he ever chase you when you leave?" I ask.

"A couple of times, but he's old and slow."

"Why do you sit up against the house?"

"They talk to me, and not at me. They treat me like a person not a kid."

"I see. Do you ever feel uncomfortable sitting here?"

"No, I love talking with them. They have some great ideas and stories to share."

"What stories?" I ask.

"Can I tell him?" she says, seemingly asking the house.

There's a brief moment of silence, and then she starts talking, "Well, there was the first time that old fart came running after me. He almost got me, but the house growled at him. He turned white and pooped his pants. Now that was funny."

"What other stories can you tell me?"

"If I tell you this one, you can't repeat this?"

"Okay, I promise I won't."

"Well, did you know that every house made after this one, before the 1960s, contained special passageways that led to this house?"

"I didn't know that. How does that work?"

"Well, in our basement, on a top shelf, you can reach into the wall and put your hand into this house."

"You mean a portal?" I state.

"I don't know what they call it. I just know I reached in and grabbed a priest's necklace and cross off him. It was cool and smelled of something rotting."

"Can you show me this portal?"

"No, my parents wouldn't allow it."

"You said there are other houses that have this?"

"Yes, they say there's at least 24 houses around here with the same secret passages where you can reach in and grab stuff."

"I see. What's your name?"

"Debbi.!"

"Well, it was great talking with you, Debbie. My name is Vincent."

"Good talking with you too."

Standing up, I can feel a cold sensation running up my spine. Walking to my car, I look back at her and smile. I get in and drive to my office.

Walking up to the building, a man stops me.

"We have to talk," he says.

"What's on your mind?" I ask.

"You're doing a story on a certain house, right?" he whispers.

"I am."

"Well, I would suggest you quit trying to get any more information."

"Why would I do that?"

"You're asking too many questions, and there are people taking notice of what you are doing."

"It's just a house with a past. Why's everyone so scared of the story getting out?"

"Damn it, man, it's not just a house! Can't you see that? This house is pure evil. People are trying to hide the house from more people coming to it and dying. The best you can do right now is quit looking for more information before something happens to you."

"Are you threatening me?" I ask.

"No, I am trying to save your life. Do you think these people haven't seen what you are doing? I am here as your last warning. Next time, you could be dead. These people aren't playing around when it comes to this house."

"Who are these people that are worried? Or don't they have the guts to show themselves?" I ask.

"You know who they are."

"The church of course."

"Yes, but there are more people connected with them. They're just the tip of the pyramid."

"Who are the others? Please, tell me."

"I can't, but if you keep probing, you'll find out soon enough."

"I guess we'll see what happens then."

"Just stupid. I have to go before they see me here with you."

"Tell me your name before you go?" I ask.

He runs quickly around the side of the building and disappears. Shaking my head, I head inside to my office. I check my messages and there are about a dozen of them waiting. Looking through them, I find one that appeals to me. I read the message: "Dear Mr. Vincent. You are looking for some answers, and I have them. Meet me at St Joseph's church tonight."

Forgotten Past

I look at my watch. There's still a couple of hours to spare before going there. I start typing what I have so far, before my watch beeps to tell me it's time time go.

I wait outside the church until I see a priest walking towards the front of it, looking around. I get out of my car and walk over to him.

"Come inside, quickly," he says, still looking around.

He opens the door and we walk in. "You're the one with answers, father?" I ask.

"Yes, my son, I am!"

He leads me to his office and closes the door quickly.

"So, what can you tell me?" I ask.

"Do you want the answers to that abomination of a house?"

"I do. What's your name?"

"Father Jacob. Not that it's going to matter anyways."

"Why's that, father?" I ask, concerned.

"As soon as anyone finds out I talked with you, I'll have a new church to serve and they'll send me far away from here."

"Is there a specific reason no one wants to talk about this house?"

"Where do I begin?

Because that house is evil. Every single board and nail; every inch of that house screams evil. That house has destroyed the lives of so many people. It eats the souls of the living. It is the opening to hell; once you go in, you don't come out. I have seen a man boarding up the back door be pulled into that house with a bloodcurdling scream, never to be seen again. That house offers you your wildest dream to get you in there and only heaven knows what happens to the poor souls after they enter. I have been here at this church for a year. I hear that house calling my name and it visits me in my dreams, tempting me, every night. Once that house gets ahold of something or someone you love, you see them every time you close your eyes. They're at the house, wanting you to come in and join them. The church is at its wits' end trying to end the evil. There's a plan in place to demolish the house and place the charred remains at hundreds of sacred grounds in and around Saskatoon."

"Why are you telling me this?" I ask.

"I am telling you because I feel the truth about this evil house must be a priority.?"

"So why are church people after me?" I ask.

"The church has undertaken containing the evil that exists, but fewer priests are willing to live across from the house. The deaths of the priests living there has taken a toll on our ranks. They want me to move in there next month. I don't want to live there, that's why I am telling you. I don't want to die."

"That makes sense now. Can you tell me about the black figure that can speak to people?"

"He is the devil. I have faced him on many occasions. Once, he came out of the house looking at me with those red eyes burning. He told me all about my future if I didn't quit sprinkling holy water all over his house. He showed me pains beyond the imagination of any human. He told me there would be a man that'd be asking about the house and that I should tell that man everything I could or that'd be my fate in life and after death. The church calls him the devil, but I think he is much more powerful than a devil. He puts into question everything we know about God and the devil. He can answer questions that could never possibly be answered, unless by a god. I believe he's a god himself."

"I can't believe I am hearing this. You believe he is God?" I answer, confused.

"Yes, how else to you explain that he can cause great pain to some while others can go up to the house and nothing happens to them?"

With nothing left for him to tell me, I stand up and walk out the door. I look back at Father Jacob and he looks terrified.

Heading back to my car, there's a man standing by the driver's door. "Excuse me?" I ask, getting closer.

"Are you that guy looking into that old Victorian house?"

"Yes, yes I am."

"You know, sometimes it's better to leave things alone that aren't meant to be talked about."

"You don't scare me."

"I don't intend on scaring you. I am just suggesting you quit looking into this. These kinds of things aren't meant to be snooped into."

"You're hoping I'll go away quietly. Who are you?"

"Let's just say I am a friend looking out for your best interest."

"Well, I have to go, friend," I reply, getting into my car.

Heading home, I decide to call it a night.

The next morning, I go into work, and am greeted by Mr. Dee.

"You're not to look into that old house anymore," he says.

"Why not? I've been working tirelessly trying to get everything I need."

"I was told to tell you to back off that story."

"But I can't! I have so much work put in…"

"Doesn't matter," he interrupts. "Come into my office for a moment, Vincent."

Walking in, Mr. Dee closes the door before continuing.

"I am only telling you this because you have never let me down on a story. I received a message yesterday from a Father Frank. He told me the church has been trying to get this house torn down. If we run the story, there are people who are going to try to stop it. Devil worshipers are going to come out of the woodwork and interfere with church business. I told him there'd be no problems with them interfering as we would run the story after the city came back with their ruling. They said we are to stop or the church will continue with legal action against us. Instead of arguing with him, I just agreed. I will tell you you have to stop, but I say keep going because if you're ticking off the church it must be something big. Can you find out more?"

"Yes, I can, but it will be hard. Yesterday I was talking to a priest and he was scared. I'll try my best not to ruffle their feathers?"

"Great, I want to see the results of this story."

"Thank you," I say, opening the door, and heading to my own office.

It's around 1 PM when I leave for lunch. I drive over to the house and stop out front. I barely get out when the priest comes out, yelling.

"Get the hell away from the house!"

"Shut up!" I shout back.

"You were told to stay away from here!"

"No. They said I can't write the story on the house, but nobody said I couldn't come by." "You get out of here or you'll pay."

"No!" I yell, grabbing his arm, and dragging him onto the property.

"Dear God! What have you done?"

"Nothing."

"You placed me on this unholy ground!"

Forgotten Past

I watch as he grabs his chest and falls to the ground. I lean down to help him, and he whispers, "help me off the grass."

I grab his arm, then remember what I had heard. That it took six people to get that woman off the grass, so I let go of his arm. I move a step back from him as the fear grows on his face. Grabbing his arm again, I try to move him off the grass. Even pulling with all my strength, he won't budge an inch. I try a couple more times, but have the same result. Looking at his face, the fear has taken over more than the heart attack. I go over to the side closer to the house and try to pick him up. I roll him over towards me, but I can't pick him up, and he is now a foot closer to the house. I stand up straight, and feel a cold breeze pass over me. Looking around, I can't see anything, but I hear laughter in the distance. I look back down at the old man and he's gone.

"What the hell happened?" I shout, turning around. I see the old man being absorbed into the outside wall.

"Help!" he screams.

I run over to him just as his leg is going through the wall. I fall back and sit there wondering, his body gone. I shake my head and keep looking, waiting for some answer to explain what I just saw.

"You know you shouldn't be that close to the house?" a woman calls from the sidewalk.

I turn to look at her, "yes, I think you're right?" I state, shocked.

I stand up, shaken, and walk over to her. "What's it about this house that strikes fear in everyone's hearts?" I ask her, looking where that old man was.

"I've heard stories, but nothing worthwhile."

"Everything is worthwhile. Would you like to talk to me about what you know?"

"Yes, I've got some time?"

"Great," I reply, walking to my car and opening the passenger side door for her. I look towards the spot where the old man disappeared and shudder, closing the door. I get in and I start driving.

"There's a great little coffee shop a few blocks from here," she says.

"That sounds perfect," I state. We pull up and go in, finding a vacant table in the corner.

"My name is Vincent."

"I'm Rachel."

"Pleasure to meet you, Rachel. I'll have a coffee and for you…?" I say as the waitress smiles.

"I'll have the same."

"What can you tell me about that house?" I ask

"Well, when I first moved into our place about 3 years ago, I was told that house was where a whole family was murdered!"

"A whole family?" I ask, shocked.

"A whole family and others. I didn't believe it either. Nobody kills a whole family without it being broadcast all over. Can I ask why you were sitting by the house?"

"I'm trying to figure out why everyone is so against the house."

"It's a weird house. I tried it, but nobody knew who the owner was. It just needs a paint job and for all those windows to be opened and un-boarded and I think it would be quite beautiful."

"Yes, it's a hell of a house," I state, looking at her.

"If you only you knew what the hell went on there, you'd run for the hills," I think to myself.

"Is something wrong? You're looking pale," Rachel asks.

"Oh, no, I'm fine. Are there any other stories you can tell me about that house?"

"Someone else said people were being pulled into the house, never to be seen again, but I think they were just playing a prank."

"Yes, that's one possibility," I reply, remembering what I just saw.

"Like I said, they are just stories I've heard, but there is one woman I've seen around there. She will usually go there and sit up against the house. I just wish that mean old man would quit chasing her. He stops when she hits the property. That's another reason I love that house, the grass is so green. Oh well, I guess we can't all get what we want."

"Yes, that's true. We have to put up with whatever comes our way."

"I've watched that girl sit there for hours on end. I guess there's a connection there."

"I saw her there once. It looked like she is talking with someone, but who knows."

"Yes, I'd say she does. She's always looking around, but it could be she's watching for that old man."

"Yes, he was grumpy?" I state.

"Did you say was?" she asks, staring at me with suspicion.

"Oh, did I? I meant he is."

"I thought maybe something happened to him."

"I don't think anything can happen to him?" I reply, faking a laugh.

"He's so grumpy I don't think the devil would want him. Anyways, I should probably get going."

"Can I give you a ride anywhere?" I ask.

"No, I'm good. My phone number is on that piece of paper. Call me sometime?"

"I will, thank you! It was a pleasure meeting you, Rachel."

I sit there, looking at her walk out the door. I stare at my coffee and think about the priest. "*How did he pass through the house like that?*" I get up and head back to work.

Later that night, I head over to the house again. As I pull up, I see a whole bunch of cars around that priest's house.

"What're you doing here?" someone shouts at me.

"Get out of here, Vincent," another man's voice calls as I step out of my car.

"What's going on?" I ask.

"None of your business."

Walking into the yard of the house, a priest comes running towards me.

"Vincent, stay away from that house! You can't be here," he yells.

"Hey, I may not be able to write the story, but you sure as hell can't tell me where I can and can't be!"

"I am warning you."

"Come get me then," I respond, confidently.

"Son, just come here. Please?" he replies, staying on the sidewalk.

I watch as the others walk across the street to join him.

"Come to the sidewalk," another man calls, holding his hand out to me.

I walk a little further towards the house.

"Look, we're trying to save your soul!"

I watch them looking at the house, and each other, trying to decide if they are going to come get me.

"That's okay. I'm just going around back if any of you want to follow me," I reply, walking to the back.

I hear their screams fade as I get closer to the back door. I turn the corner of the house and a cold breeze blows right through me. I stop in my tracks, and look around.

"You again?" a deep voice enters my ears.

"Yes, it's me," I whisper.

"What do you want this time?"

"Did you take that priest this afternoon?" I ask.

"Why's that any of your business?"

"I didn't mean to…"

"It doesn't matter if you did or didn't. He belongs to the house now. Before you try to get all teary eyed, you made a choice. Yes, I have seen many people over the years make choices that have condemned others to suffer fates worse than death. Look into the history of your kind, Vincent. Your kind has judged others for as long as you have stood on two feet. I'll never deviate on any decision I make, good or bad, as you, too, must own your own decisions.

You can never change what's done. If you kill a thousand people, you can't realize your mistake and bring them back. What you can do it not kill another person. Your kind has this atrocious behavior that what you want, you get! You don't even think for one second that you are doing anything wrong. A couple hundred thousand years and you still haven't learned you're your mistakes. I am me, I won't change a thought or a decision for anyone. You should consider your alternatives and decide how you want to live. It's your choice."

"I wish I didn't feel this bad," I answer.

"Mistakes always bear heavy weights. Your friends in front of the house want you to make a choice as well."

"I forgot about them."

"I don't feel they have forgotten about you. I'll give you a choice, and this choice is only going to happen once. You can face the mob alone, or I can get rid of them for you."

"What would you do to them?" I ask, quietly.

"I didn't say you could ask any questions. I gave you two choices, which one do you choose?"

I stand there for a moment thinking. *"If he goes after them, I'll have their deaths on my shoulders, but if I go out there, they'll kill me."* I take a deep breath and respond, "Alright, can you help me?"

"Yes, I'll help you. Just you wait," he grins.

"Wait for what?" I ask as a sudden wind blows hard, almost knocking me down. The ravenous winds blow to the front of the house, and within moments all I can hear are screams. The wind gets colder as it blows by me. A few minutes pass, and the noise lessens to a whisper. Standing right in front of me is the dark one, his eyes burning redder than before.

"Done. Don't question your decision, your choice has been made and they are gone."

"But…"

"I said don't question it."

Looking in his eyes, I answer, "Thank you."

He turns to walk away, but stop to look back. "If I were you, Vincent, I wouldn't come back here. I'd only come back when they get their way and tear this house down. One member of their group will tell the story of this house that their God damned. Once he does, the church will gain the support they need."

"I believe it's because of the killings here. They want them to be stopped?"

"What about the killing elsewhere, Vincent? They would have to destroy the whole world to stop the killing. They chose this house because they judged it necessary. The church alone is the one who wants the house torn down and buried. Think about that next time you watch what they rise up against. You'll see the side they hide from the public view. A side more evil than me. One of pain and injustice. Watch them closely."

"I will." I reply as the figure disappears into the night.

I slowly walk back to the front of the house, not knowing what to expect. There's nobody around, just my car and a few papers. I run for my car as a growl sounds from behind me. I get in and drive home quickly.

Inside my house, I start wondering, *"What did he do to those priests? Did he scare them or did he kill them?"*

It must have been around 5 in the morning when I finally get to sleep.

My phone rings at 7:38 AM. My boss Mr. Dee is telling me to cover the church vs the house. The city council has reconvened with their decision. I get ready, shoot down two cups of coffee, and head out.

Getting to city hall at 9:25 AM, I pull my notepad and recorder out, and walk towards the building. As I come to the doors, a young man stops me.

"Where do you think you're going Vincent?" he asks.

"I'm going to the council chambers," I state, watching as he tries to bulge out and make himself scarier.

"No, you're not. We need to talk."

"Well, you better make it quick," I reply.

"Why are you trying the church's patience so much? They told you to back off yet you continue to make a pain of yourself."

"Why so they want me to back me off when all I want is the truth?"

"The church has always been secretive about this house. I am sure they will tell you everything you need to know after the matter is settled."

"Do you believe they would be forthcoming? I think you're just trying to tell me what you think I want to hear. I better be heading in, it was good talking with you."

I head inside to the chambers and sit down by the podium. I watch as the church members come trickling in, a few at a time. Some look towards me, and start whispering to each other while others don't even take notice. The mayor and the council members arrive and everyone is seated.

"Hello, everyone," the mayor says, standing. "We are here to discuss the demolition of a house, brought forth by Father Daniel McAllister, and his companion church members. We could not find the land deed owner, but would like to know the specific reasons you want this house torn down. We sent a few of our administration people to the house. A few of our surveyors went there only to have a priest yelling at them as soon as they arrived. I would like to know why?"

"Your worship," Father McAllister answers. "He was trying to stop people from entering that yard for their own safety."

The mayor glares, unconvinced, as he responds louder, "I'm sorry? Yelling and chasing city officials is the church's way of helping? I guess I grew up in a different age, when they would talk with you."

"I am sorry, your worship! He was under much stress and hasn't felt well lately."

"Anyways, they found the house in satisfactory condition. The boards on the windows and doors were an eyesore, but that house just needs a paint job. Even the grass has been watered. I can't approve your demand to tear that house down."

A loud grumbling noise makes its way through the chamber.

"But, your worship. That house is evil!"

"You may see it as evil, but this house is in good shape. Since this house hasn't had people living in it for years, and no owner is available to take it over, we'll be holding an auction this coming Monday morning. We'll be putting the money made in a trust, in case an owner does come fourth. That's all ladies and gentlemen."

Everyone stands as the council leaves the chambers, and the priests start grumbling.

"You had something to do with this, didn't you Vincent?" one of them asks me.

"I had nothing to do with this. I came here because Mr. Dee asked that I be here when they gave their decision."

"If you think for one minute that you're going to buy that house, you're mistaken."

"I don't plan to buy anything. Especially not a house?"

"We are going to buy that house so you can forget about any thoughts of undermining us."

"I don't care!" I respond, feeling as if he isn't listening to a word I'm saying.

"You should not have crossed us?"

"I didn't, but seeing your true colors emerging here has made me think that religion has a lot in common with the mob."

"How dare you insult the church in that way?"

"The threats that have come my way from your church sound a lot like mobsters."

"Those "threats" as you call them are meant to save your life."

"No, those threats were meant as they sounded, to get me to back off so you and your gang could get what you wanted."

"We do God's work. What he says passes through us, and we pass it onto the people."

"Call it whatever you want, but one more threat or warning as you call it and I'll plaster every word across the front page."

"You couldn't prove it?"

"Do any of you realize I carry a recorder with me? I have every word your church members have ever said to me on tape." I respond, holding out my recorder.

"That's illegal! You can't do that?"

"I can because I report the news, and I want to make sure I get it right. Now, leave me alone."

He walks to the others and they leave, eyeing me. I pick up my notepad and head outside, back to my office to catch up on my work. I get to my office and let Mr. Dee know what happened. He tells me he might buy that house and I can't help but laugh, knowing the church is going to be mad

Monday, August 27, 1985: 8:45 AM.

We are all waiting for the auctioneer to come out. Father McAllister walks over to me and glares.

"Ah, Vincent, It's going to be a beautiful day," he says.

"Yes, I guess so."

"The church is going to love owning this house."

"You'll have to wait until it's over."

"Hi everyone, my name's Gus," the auctioneer says over the loudspeaker. "I'll be handling the auction today, so get your paddles ready. This Victorian house is in beautiful shape, I say we start the bidding at $9,000. Do I hear 9,000? I have $9,000, do I hear $10,000? I have $10,000… I have $11,000, do I hear $12,000?"

After ten-minutes of back and forth, the bidding is at $27,500.

"You can't win, Vincent," Father McAllister says, fuming.

"I'm not bidding," I state, confused.

"You came with him, stop him from bidding!" he says, looking towards Mr. Dee.

"Yes, I did, because he's my boss!" I answer, annoyed.

"Well, do something to stop him from bidding."

"I'm not getting involved," I reply.

Father McAllister walks away from me and towards another man, pointing at my boss. The bid is at $31,250. The other man walks over to Mr. Dee and says something quietly in his ear. Mr. Dee raises the bid to $40,000."

"Say one more word to me and I'll raise it to $60,000," I hear him say.

The bid is $41,125, and the priests look annoyed. When the bidding ends, it's an astonishing $83,350, won by the priests who aren't one bit happy. We walk away but Father McAllister comes up to us.

"Good try, but the church always wins," he gloats.

"I didn't want to win, I just wanted to see how bad you wanted it," Mr. Dee replies.

"We spent all the church's funds for this house. A house you don't even want?"

"Yes, and you have a great looking house! If you want to sell it to me, I'll buy it for $40,000 right now."

"Never. We can finally get rid of that damned house forever."

"Too bad. That's a good-looking house. Enjoy it," Mr. Dee shrugs.

We walk away and I can hear the father cursing us both.

September 12th, 1985

My phone rings at 6:23 AM. Mr. Dee is telling me to get over to that house,

"They are going to demolish the house, and they are bringing everything!"

I'm dressed in ten minutes and racing over there. They have the street blocked off and full of bulldozers and dump trucks blessed with holy water. At least a hundred priests are praying across the street. I start writing down what I am seeing.

At 9:30, the bulldozer heads towards the house slowly, lifting its blade. It hits the house and stops. The engine revs up but goes nowhere. I swear I can hear the house scream, as if it were calling for help. The bulldozer finally breaks through the right front corner and a few priests come running, throwing holy water where it's broken through. A board flies off and hits a priest in the face, sending him to the ground. Another one takes his place as the bulldozer creeps in even further. Another priest disappears, as if the house pulled him in. Wrecking balls head towards the house and the priests back away quickly.

The ball raises above the house, and drops on the top. It takes seven tries before the house falls in on itself. The priests come running, throwing holy water again. They surround the remaining debris. A loader starts moving towards the house with a dump truck, and the house slowly starts to disappear, one truckload at a time.

"Where they are taking it?" I ask a spectator.

"They are going to burn the pieces on hallowed ground, and put what can't be burned into graves. These pieces will go to cemeteries, buried in their own graves I'm guessing?"

"That's a lot of work."

"Yes, but it will contain the evil forever!"

I walk back to my car and watch as the house continues to shrink with each dump truck leaving.

By the next morning, there's a ten-foot hole where the property was, and the priests continue to throw holy water, waterlogging the ground.

"God wins again!" I hear them say.

I start my car and head to work to write my story. I talk to Mr. Dee and let him know what happened and what I heard before I head to my office, saddened by what I saw.

I sit at my desk and wonder what happened to all the people that died there. Are they free or gone forever? I look out my window, seeing the sun shining brightly as it always has. I think of what the dark one said to me, "The house God damned" and start writing.

THE HOUSE GOD DAMNED

I saw the demolition of a house yesterday. A house riddled with mysteries and wonders. A house that's been standing for more than a hundred years. One church wanted the house gone, while others enjoyed its serenity. I spoke with many priests and they wouldn't talk about much. Other people I spoke with had many tales to tell. I cannot see why they went to so much expense to destroy the beauty that was that house. I do not see why they couldn't find it in their hearts to forgive. Yes, people have passed away there, but what's next? I feel a great sadness for the community that lost a part of their heritage.

I put my pen down and lean back in my chair. I grab the pad of paper and head to the editor's office to drop it in his inbox.

A call wakes me up and I reach for the phone. A priest wants to meet up at Kinsmen Park. I get ready and head over there. There is a cool chill in the air and the grey skies above say the snow will fall soon. Thirty minutes go by before I see an old man wearing a black overcoat and a hat coming towards me.

"You must be Vincent," he responds.

"Yes, and you are?"

"My name is no concern of yours. I am here as a favor to father Francis. He's the one who talked to you before. I took his confession before he passed last week. He wanted to make sure his soul was going to heaven. I just wanted to let you know that he passed and I wanted to ask why are you causing so much trouble for the church."

"I was just following a story."

"Well, I guess the story is done?"

"Yes, it's done."

He tips his hat at me and walks up to the path, disappearing. I head back to the office, trying to figure out why he just wanted to tell me that. Sitting in my chair, I reach into the file cabinet and pull out the files on the house. Opening the folder, there's nothing there. All my work is gone! I stand up and head to Mr. Dee's office and knock on the door.

"Come in Vincent, how's it going today?" he says, opening the door.

"Someone stole my files on the house!" I blurt out.

"What do you mean someone stole the files?"

"I mean they are all gone!" I shout.

"Were other files missing?"

"I don't know, I'll go check right now."

"No, don't worry. They got what they wanted. They have wanted the story about the house you were doing. It's my fault, I should have made copies. Just go back to work and I'll deal with them."

Epilogue

This story is based on the point of view from five people who experienced this house. Each person gave his or her version of the events they witnessed over the years while the Victorian house stood. I was doubtful in the beginning as my only experiences with the house was having my BMX front wheel stop turning while going down the three sisters' hill. After hearing these people out, I truly believe there is more than just a haunted house that occupied that lot. Although they had different opinions of what they thought, putting their words together made for an interesting tale of events. The people who gave their stories requested anonymity, fearing repercussions. As per their wishes, they were each given a copy of the story once finished, and I was given their approval to publish. This house creates one question: does evil leave after a place is gone, or does it stick around and wait for another home to be built in its place?

The End

Forgotten Past

The Furnace. What does a greedy realtor have in common with unsuspecting families? A 19th-century factory that was converted into a family home in the 1940s. Gerald Kent, owner of We Care Home Reality has a villainess plan. It will see sales soar, but at what cost?

The Sanatorium. A night of passion leads to death for some, and nightmares for others. Amy Cruz tries to find two of her friends that disappear while on a date at the Sanatorium. She soon discovers horrendous secret about a doctor who is still on call.

Stranger in a Strange Land. Annabelle Church is a sixteen-year-old with a problem. She was flung through time from 1945 to 2000 and quickly discovered people are not always as they seem. After enduring some of the worst torture imaginable, Annabelle finds her way home only to find out she is a messenger of death.

The House God Damned. A Victorian house with a deadly beginning continues to leave a trail of dead. Vincent, a reporter, goes up against the mighty church in a fight where only one side can win. The church wants the house to vanish into nothingness but Vincent wants to learn more about the evil contained within.

Pankratz

In loving memory of Crystal Douglas, taken way too soon from this world. I was/am proud to call you friend. When we first met in the smoking area at SIAST in 2013, you were annoyed with your bus not having showed up after an hour of waiting. I just couldn't walk by, instead, I brought my bad sense of humor, and stayed until you were smiling again. We've been friends since that day.

The last time I saw you seems like a thousand years ago, but was actually on graduation day, May, of 2014. A day your smile was never ending. I'm just glad I was a part of your life for those five years, but now I'm left with memories, and I'll cherish those with every ounce of my being.

Rest in Peace my friend.